TEARS IN THE MIST

A novel based on historical events

GEORGIOS VENGKA - MARGARITIS

GEORGIOS VENGKA - MARGARITIS

TABLE OF CONTENTS

THIS ISN'T RIGHT

He lay on the bed, his eyes wide open. There was a slight hum coming from the ceiling fan above, its blades moving slowly in unison. Other than that, it was quiet. At least inside his room. He could hear the faint sound of the children as they trooped back from school.

He loved peace a lot. He loved the calm, and quietness which he had. Until the call ran through from the next room.

"George! George! Where on bloody earth is that idiot?" the female voice called loudly.

With a defeated sigh, George stood up. He was about 6'2" (1.88cm), a height he inherited from his father. He had a lean built which he had also inherited from his father. His hair was a black wave, gotten from both of his Greek parents. His face was handsome, his eyes black, his nose brisk, with high cheekbones flaunting both sides of his cheeks. However, his eyes, which were said to be the doorway to the soul, looked tormented. He avoided staring at himself in the mirror because of what he could see in them.

"George!"

"I'm coming," he called as he hurried out the door.

He walked down the dark hallway into a fairly bright living room. It was heavily furnished with several red couches which were a dark contrast to the brown rug on the ground. It was a simple living room, the flat TV screen being the only exorbitant fixture.

"Mama," he said quietly, his eyes on the only other occupant in the room, the woman who sat on a couch, her feet placed on a table, her eyes on the TV screen, and the remote in her hand.

4

Alessandra still remained beautiful, but she had once been extremely beautiful. The colored pictures on the walls were evidence of the fact. They showed her smiling, holding on to a beautiful man who smiled back at her. George could not recall when last he had seen her smile at him; it had to be several years ago when he had been a little boy. Now, all that filled her face were frowns, and sneers, all directed at him. Her hair was black, just like his, and always packed into a bun. Her face was in her usual fixture, which over the years was now filled with more lines and wrinkles. She was a shadow of herself, a shadow of the woman he had to call his mother.

She ignored him as he stood there, a cackle emanating from her lips as a scene came up on the screen. He remained there, he knew what could happen if he left. The remote might as well leave a scar on his head. He grimaced as he thought of the last time it had happened, he still had a scar to the effect, and once in a while, he could feel the searing pain.

He stood there for what seemed to be twenty minutes, then she turned her eyes to him as if just seeing him there for the first time. "Go make lunch," she said with a wave of her hand, her eyes back on the TV.

"What would you like to eat for lunch mama?" he asked.

She was quiet once again. This time around, it took her even longer to answer him, yet he remained, scared of the repercussions if he should walk away.

"Ribs," she said, her eyes glued to the TV.

"Yes, mama." He walked away with a heavy heart, hoping she would not call him back for walking off when she wasn't done with him. It was only when he got into the kitchen that he let out a sigh of relief. He went straight to preparing lunch. It was no hard chore. He had been doing so ever since he was nine years old.

In a few minutes, the aroma drifted all over the kitchen as George cooked. His eyes were attentive as he stared at the ribs which were in the pan. They had to be done the right way. Just a second and they could be overcooked, which would be bad for him. He flipped the ribs to the other side and made sure they were golden brown, just the way his mother loved them.

"Food is ready mama," he announced as he placed her plate on the dining table.

"Are you too stupid to not know that you should bring my food to me?" his mother snapped, a glare on her face.

"I'm sorry mama," George said, as he took the plate to her. He closed his eyes as he laid the plates in front of her, anticipating the slap. It didn't happen. When he opened his eyes, she had a smile on her face, one which filled him with chills. His mother's smile was never good! As he walked away, he squealed. Her hand grabbed his arm, with her sharp fingers digging into him.

"Mama!" he cried, as her fingers dug deeper into his skin.

"Why am I surprised that you have no sense? You're such a mistake. I should have aborted you, or better still, murdered you in your sleep. Now all you do is eat my food. Bastard!" she spat as her fingers drew blood.

"Mama please," George cried.

His pleas only infuriated her more, driving all her claws into his skin. She cared for her looks, but she cared the most for her fingernails that she made weekly on a parlor, just for the purpose of inflicting pain on him, George couldn't figure out another reason for this. He gasped as she twisted them into his skin. A tear escaped his eyes, and then another. It was only then she let go, pleased with what she had seen.

"Hide somewhere, I don't want to see you for the rest of the day," Alessandra said, her attention turned again to the TV screen.

The pain filled his arm as he hurried to the kitchen. Hurrying, he dished the leftover of the meal which wasn't much into a plastic plate then dashed into his room before his mother could decide to come to the kitchen. He looked at his arm. Sure enough, he could see blood and the bruise on his tanned skin. He grabbed a cotton wool and patted it on it, soaking up the blood on the surface.

His appetite was gone, he decided as he looked at the plate. But he needed to eat the meal, every single bit. She would check his plate, as well as the dustbin to see if there was any leftover, and if there was, he would pay dearly for it.

Alessandra Rossi had not always been this way. Sure she was never the loving and caring mother all children deserve but George still had faint memories of happier times. He could still recall faintly his mother smiling, her hands on his sides as she tickled him. He could still remember the delicious aroma as she placed the plate of spaghetti in front of him. He could still remember how she used to take care of him when he was sick. And then were the moments when she was quiet towards him, when she just wanted to be left alone, but she almost always tried to make up for it. But then, everything had changed with the divorce.

He had been just six years old when it happened. He would never forget. He would always remember the yelling. He had woken up from a nap to hear his mother shouting at his father. He had been young but he understood the meaning of the words being thrown at him.

"Bastard! How could you do such a thing! Bastard!" his mother had yelled as she slammed against his father's chest.

George had always loved his father more than his mother. Antonio was a man with a smile always, who always ruffled his hair. He was not always home because of his work but whenever he was, he made sure to buy something for George, toys or sweets, and take the family out.

"You need to calm down Alessandra! George is asleep!" Antonio had said.

"Asleep? He should know that his father is nothing but a dog! That's what you're! A dog who can't keep his wandering dick to himself!"

"Calm down Alessandra! You should have known this would happen. Our marriage is not the same as it used to be. We should never have married. All I want is a divorce," Antonio said.

"No! You can't leave me! You can't!" Alessandra cried, bashing her fists against her husband's chest.

A scared George had run in, trying to separate his parents whom he had never seen them fight.

"Papa! Mama! Please don't fight!" George cried.

His mother turned to him with tears in her eyes. "Your papa wants to leave us, George, your daddy wants to leave us!"

Tears of his own began to fall, as George thought of his father leaving them. His father was always protecting him from his mother rages and the thought of being alone and helpless terrified him. "Papa, please don't go. Papa please, don't leave us."

His father had only looked at him with sadness in his eyes, then he had grabbed a suitcase and left. What followed next, little George had been a party to. There had been no stopping his father who wanted out of the marriage and wanted a divorce. He didn't want custody of George and

Alessandra would try to make his life as miserable as possible. He was leaving, but she would make him pay a monthly allowance. George hadn't been exposed to court hearings and they didn't even know how these proceedings worked. They only realized that custody had been granted to his mother, with their father being allowed to take them to his new house at weekends and pay to their mother a heavy monthly child support.

The divorce had changed his mother totally. For weeks after the divorce, she had held on to the notion that it was all her husband's fault and that he would beg her to return. Her rages were now much more common. Even when she prepared meals for her two kids, she was swearing and cursing her husband. At one of her many fits of rage, she put all of his clothes from the wardrobe in a big pile and threw them from her porch.

Over the years, her state began to worsen. She stopped caring for George who began to take over the responsibilities as the man of the house, or as his mother was saying mocking him as the maid of the house. He did the domestic chores and ran the errands. As he began to grow up, looking more like his father, her hatred for him began to grow vast. He was a reminder of his father, and she despised him, blaming him for the divorce. "If we hadn't had you, we would still be together," she had said. "You didn't fight to keep your papa, you couldn't even beg your father to stay! You wanted him to leave didn't you?" she had yelled one afternoon, throwing her shoes his way. Nothing he said could make her change her mind that he was cut off the very coat as his father.

For more than fourteen years, he had been enduring her ill-treatment. She abused him verbally, physically, and physiologically, not letting go, at least for the moment until she saw the pain of her acts reflect in him. But it was never enough, and she did all she could to make life miserable for him.

He hated it. He hated the way she treated him. But even more, he hated his life. But he could not fight her. Why should he? Even though she said some of the things she did out of hatred, they had to be true. He had not been able to keep his father. The same father who had stopped sending checks or visiting a long time ago. The same father who had remarried two times after divorcing his mother. His mother was right; there was something in him which drove others away. First, he had driven his father away, and now his mother. Besides George didn't know that his life wasn't normal cause it has been this way since he was a child. He thought all children had similar lives and struggles. He took him too long to realize that all this wasn't normal, that he deserved to be treated with respect.

He could not leave her either. She was the only family he had, and he could not leave her alone, just as his father had done. Besides, where would he go? At twenty-one, he had barely graduated with good grades, and going off to college was impossible since his mother would rather burn whatever money she had, than waste it on a nonentity like him. It was fine with him, he wasn't one for education. So he spent the little knowledge and skill he had working as a cashier at a local grocery shop and keeping the grounds of the church where he found solace in.

With all the travails he went through, the church was his home. It was where he could run to and feel at peace before he walked out the doors and was visited with the harsh realities of life. George's mother was never a woman of the church but his grandmother was. He could remember the Sundays at the summer holidays that he used to spend at his grandparent's village when his grandmother would wake him up to go with her to church and sit together in the front pew. He had always been captivated by the melodious hymn and the formalities of the priesthood. At ten, he had become an altar boy, helping the priest with the morning mass as he held the censer. His mother tried many times to pull him away from the church after the divorce, the fact that George was so calm and happy there just make her angry. She hated the church for that even blaming God about whatever was going wrong at her life, but George would never leave, it was the only thing which gave him happiness in the cold dark world.

He closed his eyes as he perched on the bed, the plate in front of him empty. His arm still ached, and he knew there would be a mark there, just as the several marks he had on different parts of his body. There was the one on his buttocks which he had gotten when he was just a little boy, and his mother flogged him butt naked with a belt which had a strong steel buckle. There was the one on the side of his eye which he had gotten when she threw her shoe at him, and the heel narrowly escaped his eye.

At times, he felt like stopping her. He felt like yelling back at her, or holding her hand when she tried to hurt him, but then he remembered, "Children, obey your parents". It was commanded by God, and even though his mother was hurting him, it would only make things worse if he chose to fight her. He had done so a few times, and he knew how cruel she could be, going the extra mile to make sure that he paid for his stubbornness. The best thing he could do was pray. Pray for her. Pray that she would see that he was different from his father, he was here for her, and he was not leaving. Yes, the only thing he could do was pray.

IN THE NAME OF THE FATHER

"In the name of the Father, and the son, and the Holy Spirit. Amen."

The words flowed from George' mouth along with the other patrons of the St. Andrew's parish. The mass was in full attendance, and as the service came to an end, there was an outflow out of the building. George remained seated, his head lowered as he murmured extra prayers. Most of all, he prayed for his mother, hoping that the good Lord would not only protect her but also make her love him. He had been doing this prayer since he was a boy, and he would never stop praying. One day, this prayer of his would be answered, and he would not stop the chance of it been granted, by hating his mother or ceasing to pray for her.

"George."

He opened his eyes and looked up, into the kind eyes of Father Lazarus. The priest was an old man in his early sixties, who had been at the church since forever. He had been the one to baptize George.

"Father," George said, bowing his head out of respect.

"How are you George?" the priest asked.

Another thing which George loved about the church was the care of the body of the church as a whole. They fed, they clothed, and they loved. They didn't ask questions, but they had warm, welcoming arms to anyone, and George had been a recipient several times. When he had been left hungry by his mother, he could always count on a warm meal at the rectory. Whenever she didn't want to behold him, he could always spend a day or two on the pews of the church without being thrown out. The church had taught him the true meaning of love, and for this, he would always be grateful.

"I'm faring well Father. Thank you," George said politely. There was so much he wanted to tell the priest. That he would rather not go home. That he had not had a decent food in days because his mother felt he was eating too much, even if he barely ate one or two times a day. But he kept his mouth closed, just as he had done since he was a little boy with no explanation for the scars on his bodies as the priest questioned him.

"Have you had breakfast?"

His stomach chose to rumble at that moment, and the priest burst into a robust laugh, which George joined in. Putting a hand over George, the priest said, "So have I. Let's go have a breakfast George before the worms in your stomach start a revolt."

The meal was simple, just as the priests at the parish were, but it was more than enough for George who had not eaten since the previous day. He ate quickly the slices of bread which were covered in jam and drank down the warm milk which was produced from cows at farms of Greece.

"Do you want more?" the priest asked, looking at him from behind his glasses.

A blush spread over his face, and he said, "I don't..."

"Don't worry George, you can have some more," the priest insisted.

George was more than happy to have another round of breakfast, but this time he ate slowly, seeming to remember his manners.

"When was the last time that you had any news from your father?" the priest asked.

George froze. The priest, God bless his kind soul, had also been the one to baptize Antonio, George's father. He had also tried to intercede during the divorce. George could remember the times he had been dragged by his mother to the church. All the sessions had ended with her weeping, and throwing herself on the ground, with his father walking away with a grim look, wondering why he had come in the first place. However, the kind priest who was loved by all could not save the marriage.

"I can't recall," George mumbled, pushing a mouthful of bread into his mouth. At times, he despised his father, for leaving him, for not fighting hard for him, rather than leaving him with his mother, and for abandoning him all this while. And other times? He considered his father a lucky man. He had escaped, without looking back, the clutches of his mother. However, he would always be mad at him for being the catalyst who had made his mother the woman who she was today.

The last time he had seen his father had been ten years ago. February 7th, which had been his birthday. He had been looking forward to that day, and the moment he woke up, he was well dressed, looking out the window as he waited for his father, his mother giving him angry looks. He had thought nothing would ruin the day, well, until his father had arrived. The first minutes had been quite okay, his mother quiet, with nothing but a dreamy smile as she had her family together once again. Everything changed when his father decided to take him out to have dinner, just the two of them alone, the birthday boy and his father.

Alessandra had refused vehemently. "You won't be taking him with you unless I go with you!" she had snapped.

"But, he's my son. I am not going to run off with him. We're just going to have dinner," his father defended.

"Then take me with you!" Alessandra pushed.

14

However, Antonio was having none of it. He wasn't going to be blackmailed into tolerating his ex-wife. He had tried to take George with him, but Alessandra began to scream, pulling at her son who was in near tears at the sight of his parents fighting on such a special day.

"I won't do this anymore!" Antonio yelled as he stormed out of the house, the door banging behind him.

All he left was a wrapped gift which George held to himself. In his room, his eyes filled with tears, he unwrapped the gift his father had bought for him. First was the singing card, which when he opened sang 'Happy Birthday', causing him to wipe the tears away. Then he had pulled out the yellow big car which had made a smile spread on his lips. He loved the car instantly and began to move it on the ground, making a vroom - vroom sound.

The door opened and he looked up at his mother, hoping that she had come to apologize, to tell him that he could go with his father without her. Instead, she had lunged for the card, staring at him with hate.

"Nooo!!" George had screamed as she tore the card into pieces. She pushed him away as the pieces of the dying singing card fell to the ground. His eyes went to the yellow truck, and as he dived for it, she was on to him.

"You stupid boy!" Alessandra yelled as she fought for the truck with him, digging her fingers into his skin as he cried. "He came for you! Only you! He has forgotten about me! He no longer gives me gifts. No more! No more! I gave birth to you, I should receive gifts, not you."

She tossed him on the bed and he cried as he watched the unforgettable scene before him. She smashed the truck on the ground several times, her heels crashing on it as she destroyed it. When she was done, it was in ruins, and his face was soaked with tears. It was the worst day of his life, at least he thought so.

That was officially the last day he had seen his father. He could not even remember the few times his father had dropped by in school, and how awkward it had been. Then, his father had told him barely a year later after the divorce that he was getting married. He had wanted George to meet his new wife and to attend the wedding. Oh, how Alessandra had laughed when a naïve George told her of his plans to be at his father's wedding. A few minutes later, he was crying in his room, both sides of his face red with the slaps received from his mother. Needless to say, he had never gone for the wedding, nor had he seen his stepmother.

Over the years, he had lost touch with his father. There were no calls, there were no cards, and his father was merely a stranger to him. If George wasn't stalking his father once in a while on social media, if he saw him on the road, he would have no idea who he was. George had three new siblings from his stepmother, three sisters who looked so much like their father – his father. From what he saw, his father had forgotten totally about him, choosing to shower all his love and attention to his new family.

"Have you thought about paying him a visit?" the priest asked.

He would never do that. Not after his father had abandoned him. Besides, he knew what awaited him if he visited his father. The man would turn him back, telling him to go back to his mother. And when he would return, oh boy! He had no idea how she did it, she seemed to have some sixth sense, but Alessandra would know where he had gone to, and when he returned home, hell would be waiting. It definitely wasn't worth it.

"No, I don't want to see him, and I don't think he wants to see me either," George said.

The priest sighed. "You should try to see him, he still remains your father."

16

"I don't know about that anymore," George said looking away. He despised his father for what he had done, for tearing their family apart. During his teen years, he had lived with bullying from his classmates who taunted him for having no father. He had felt so insecure and he still did. Seeing kids with their fathers had made him feel some sort of emptiness. Seeing fathers playing with their kids made him think that he never had a parent to teach him how to play ball or someone to talk to him about the birds and the bees. He had not had a father figure the time he needed him. And now, he didn't think he wanted him back. That ship had long sailed.

The priest was quiet, then he nodded. "Forgiveness is important my son."

"I know father, and I do forgive him, but... so much has happened. Can we let this be?"

The priest must have seen the devastated look on his face because he changed the topic. When George left the rectory, he left with a basket of freshly baked pastries and some soup which he was grateful to have.

Closing the door behind him, he was glad to see his mother passed out on the couch, bottles of beer littered below her. Quietly, he tiptoed past her, keeping the basket under his bed, where hopefully she would not find it. Then he returned to the living room, he packed the bottles, scrunching his nose at the stale smell. He hated how much she drank. The money she could spend on other useful things, she wasted on drinks. He believed it made her even bitterer. But he didn't have the courage to tell her so. He had once tried to pass the message across to her by draining the contents of the bottles into the toilet, and it had caused him to go days without food.

As he stood up, her hand latched out at him. He froze, fearing for the worse. Her eyes opened drowsily and she glared at him, as her fingers

17

dug into his skin. "Just like your bloody father, never amount to anything," she said.

The words hit him hard. He knew she was right. He would never amount to anything in life. Her hand slid away, and her eyes closed, her loud snores filling the room. It was with a heavy heart he walked away.

SUDDEN CHANGES

The front door opened ushering in a group of teenagers giggling. The boys were dressed in shorts, and flowery shirts, while the girls were dressed in breezy gowns. They all looked like they had come from the beach, or were headed there.

As they giggled and talked, George's eyes were fixed on them. Oh, the joy of youth. He envied them. They got to spend the time on one of the beaches which Greece was filled with. He loved the beach, at least he remembered so, from the few times when he had visited with his family as a child. However, as an adult, he never went to the beach. He had no time for such fun. Or perhaps he did but had no one to go with. At least, he could smell the waves and feel the wind whenever he was close to one.

As a teen, he had never had many friends, especially after the divorce when everything had fallen apart for him. He had become more of a recluse, with him bullied by the kids who considered him strange. Now, he just had two or three friends, and even with that, he was not really close to them. None of them knew of the struggles he was going through, and perhaps this had to do with him not inviting them home, he knew how much his mother would embarrass him if he did so.

"Hey! How are you doing?"

He looked up from the cashier to a bright-eyed girl with black long hair. She had come with the crowd, and he could see a pair of black bikini underneath her gown. She was pretty and was smiling widely at him.

"Hey," George said, quickly looking down at the cashier machine.

"How has been your day? Lots of work to do?" the girl continued.

"I guess so. What are you getting?" George said.

The girl sighed and pushed a basket at him. There was barely anything in it, just a few wraps of chocolate which he added up and gave to her. She called out to her friends, and as they walked out the door, their eyes were trained on him.

A slap descended on his back and he turned around to Chris. Chris was a short, brisk looking guy who George had a love-hate relationship with. He was a crude guy, not mindful of the foul words which came out of his mouth. He always seemed to shock George. At the same time, he could be quite reasonable.

"You're so freaking daft!" Chris said, shaking his head.

"Huh?"

"Couldn't you see that she was flirting with you?"

"Me?" George asked with a confused frown.

Chris sighed. "You're such a case. Haven't you noticed she always comes around with her friends, and barely buys anything? That's called flirting buddy."

"I don't think so," George disagreed.

Chris threw his hands up. "I give up my friend. You fucking have no idea that chicks flirt with you. What are you a virgin?" Chris chuckled at his private joke as he walked away.

Chris was not far from the truth, he was actually right on the mark. George was a virgin at twenty-one. The closest thing to a sexual encounter had been a kiss and touching Maria's back when he was fourteen at one of the rare occasions he went to a birthday party of one of his school friends. His shyness prevented him from making any move towards the opposite sex. He could barely exchange a few words with a girl without stuttering. It

20

wasn't as if he hadn't liked any girl before, but whenever he wanted to make an advance, the words just got stuck in his throat, making him a babbling idiot, or a mute. One day, hopefully, he would be able to get over the shyness he felt towards women.

By three in the afternoon, it was his time to close and for the evening shift to begin. He mumbled a goodbye to Chris and headed out. Today was one of those days he was not going home directly; he decided he wanted to catch up with a friend of his, Anton. Both boys had been friends since kindergarten, and Anton had been with him all through the divorce of his parents. Perhaps, Anton was able to relate more to him since his parents were divorced, however, his parents had a cordial relationship, and he got to spend time with his father. While they were good friends, Anton, however, didn't know of the abuse George had been going through for most of his life. It was a part of him he never told anyone.

The Dolans stayed in a modest storey building whose lawn was covered with beautiful roses, courtesy of Mrs. Dolan who took her garden seriously. She was the one who opened the door when he knocked.

"Hello Mrs. Dolan," he said quietly.

She smiled at him, pulling him in for a hug which made him stiffen like he did all the time. It felt so strange to be hugged, but Mrs. Dolan was that sort of person, and there was always a hug waiting for him here.

"You need some food George, I can see your bones sticking out your hollow face," Mrs. Dolan teased. "Doesn't your mama cook for you?" she asked more seriously.

George chuckled nervously. "She does."

"Now that I talk about her, how is she? I haven't seen her in a long while. Like she fell off the face of the earth," Mrs. Dolan continued.

"I will send her your regards," George said. His mother had cut off almost everyone who had been friends with his father, one of which had been Mrs. Dolan. She had just left a few friends, whom she was always hostile towards, but he doubted they really knew how cruel his mother was. Her life was quite simple; she was either at work where she was a court clerk, at home or at a beauty salon. She didn't even date, rejecting all the men who dared to ask her out. One time, she had thrown a bucket of water on a suitor when he came calling to the house with flowers. He wished she would move on, find a new man to love and care for. He thought and hoped that if she managed to establish a new relationship his troubles would end and they would both be happy.

"Good. Good. You tell her I asked for her, and maybe one of these days, I will drop by," Mrs. Dolan said.

He hoped she didn't drop by. He was sure his mother would shut the door in her face. He walked up the stairs, and down the hall to where he knew Anton would be. He knocked twice on the door of his bedroom, before walking in.

Anton was a tall and lanky kid, it seemed like he never stopped growing. He looked up from his computer with a smile as George walked in.

"Hey, buddy! Where have you been? I thought aliens captured you or something," Anton teased.

George grinned as he sat on the bed. Looking around Anton's room, it was a huge contrast to his. Here, it looked like it was well lived. Anton was not afraid to express himself on the wallpapers, and the splash of bright colors was all over. Everywhere in the room looked taken with books, a shelf, or other personal belongings of Anton. George could not do such a thing in his almost bare room. He had once tried wallpapering his room, using his savings to buy some wallpaper from a tool shop. He had barely covered a wall when his mother burst into his room, tearing the papers off the wall. He lived like a stranger at his home, as if one day, he could be thrown out of the house.

"Just been occupied with work, and church," George said.

"One would think you work for the presidency and not in some grocery shop and an old church," Anton said, rolling his eyes.

"It's not an old church," George defended.

"Yeah right."

There was a pause of silence as Anton paid attention to the computer screen, his fingers typing rhythmically on the keyboard.

"What are you doing?" George asked.

"Filing some form for a scholarship," Anton answered.

"Oh," was only what George could say. He was not surprised Anton was thinking of furthering his education. The finances were there, and so was the drive on Anton's part. After high school, he had done a little program in the community college, and after some deliberation, he was thinking of going to a standard university.

"You know, you can always change your mind about going to school," Anton said.

George chuckled. Yeah right. Who would sponsor his studies in the first place? Definitely not his mother who had told him point blank when he had graduated that she wasn't going to waste any more funds on his education. He wasn't intelligent to bag a scholarship either. What he needed to do was work, and not be stuck in the four walls of school which he knew he would hate. He had barely passed through high school, and now advanced education? He wasn't up for that.

Anton swirled his chair around, his arms folded as he stared at his good friend.

"What?" George asked.

"What are you going to do with your life man?"

George shrugged. "I don't know. I have a job right now."

"Which doesn't pay shit. Are you going to live on that for the rest of your life? And when you have a family? The same old shit? Man, you got to have dreams or ambitions, or something."

George looked away, his eyes filled with lost dreams. At six, he had wanted to be a fireman when he had watched on TV a fire that razed several buildings. Seeing those people cry on TV had made him want to be a fireman who would save lives and buildings. At that same age, he had wanted to be a priest, so he could talk to God and answer people's prayers. At eight, he had wanted to be a doctor so he could save lives. At twelve, he had wanted to be a teacher, so he could help kids, and stop them from being bullied. And now? He didn't want to be anything. Why would he dream, when it would never come true? It was just fruitless and would only cause him pain. He was content with the job he was doing, and although he knew Anton was right, this job would not be able to keep him forever, he would stick to it until life made changes.

"You could travel you know. Around the world," Anton said, his voice filled with excitement.

"With what money?" George asked.

"Well, that's right. But you should do something that you like. Time waits for no man you know. We all need to upgrade our lives," Anton said.

"So you're really leaving? I thought you didn't want to go off to college," George said.

Anton shrugged. "I thought over it long and hard. I want to make something out of myself, a name, a profession. I'm young, and now is the time to do what I want with my life. Besides, who's going to pay my bills? Or care for my mom? That's all on me."

"And where are you thinking of going to?"

"There's a university in Thessaloniki that I am interested into," Anton said.

George's heart fell. Thessaloniki was quite a stretch from Athens. "You're leaving?"

Anton laughed. "One would think you were my girlfriend with that look on your face. Come on, I'm not dying, just going over to Thessaloniki. There's a great private University there, and their scholarship covers a lot. It's a conducive place for learning."

"What about your mother? She's going to be alone."

"Ha! I wish. She has all my aunties, and the many friends she needs. This house is going to be busy when I leave, I assure you."

"When will you be leaving? Any time soon?"

"A few months from now. It won't be hard to get in. I got good grades."

George was almost terrified. Anton was going to be moving away. Off to college. He could already see their relationship coming to an end. There had to be tons of people in the university, and in no time, he would forget about his friend who was working at a grocery shop with no hopes of going to university. He had never thought he would lose Anton or their friendship, but it was inevitable with Anton leaving.

"I'm going to miss you, friend. You know you could come with me. We're going to have mad fun in Thessaloniki," Anton said excitedly, already seeing himself in the new city.

"You know I have responsibilities here," George excused.

"Yeah right," Anton said dryly. He took from the side of the table a few pamphlets which he dashed at George. They were pamphlets of different universities. A few were of schools in Greece, while others were of schools outside the country. He flipped through one of a college in the United States.

"I was thinking of leaving the country. Going off to Canada or USA, but my mother was having none of it. So we reached a compromise on Thessaloniki. But I tell you, out of the country will be more fun. I heard their girls are crazy and more beautiful. Hmm…" Anton said dreamily.

George stopped at a pamphlet. It was one of a university in Sydney, Australia. It was captivating, the background of the countryside surrounded by beaches. The students looked happy as if they wanted to be there. "If I wanted to go to college, I would choose Australia," George said.

Anton rolled his eyes. "Australia? That's boring. No girls with skimpy outfits there. But I heard it's cool. They got infrastructures and everything. I think you will find it great there, boring just like you."

As George made the walk home, he was in deep thoughts. He could not believe Anton was leaving, but that was how Anton was. He had big dreams and didn't care if others were going to be affected. To be honest, he was probably the only one that was going to be truly affected by Anton's absence. He had only a few friends, but he did not have a bond with them as he did with Anton, and now his best pal was leaving. It would just be him in the world. The thought made him choke on his tears. Everyone was just leaving him. First his dad, then his mother, and now Anton. It was either a messed up world or something had to be wrong with him.

He cleaned the escaped tears before he walked into the house. As he walked past the door, he jumped, dodging the slippers which were thrown at him. His mother sat on the couch, glaring at him, with hatred in her eyes. "Where have you been?"

"I was with Anton mama," George said, as he backed against the wall.

"Anton! He's your excuse right! Your father used to use his friends as excuses while he whored around. Shameless friends, just like your Anton!" Her eyes widened. "You must have been with a woman. Yes, you were with one! How many do you have now! You think you're some man now? So you can screw around with those women? Whispering sweet words into their ears!"

He shook his head in defense. "No mother, I went to see Anton. I don't have any woman!"

A plate which was on the center table headed towards his direction, narrowly missing him.

"Don't you dare lie to me!" his mother yelled waving her finger. "You're just like your father. A bloody liar! Bastards! You told her you loved her, didn't you! You told those poor women you loved them!"

27

She began to move towards him, and he began to edge away, against the wall, her eyes filled with anger, directed at him. Before he could leap away, she descended on him, raining blows on him. He covered his head with his hands, his eyes shut close, as her heavy hands continued to beat hard on him. It seemed to last forever, the ordeal. Then she stopped, taking deep breaths.

"Bastards," she mumbled as she walked away.

With wobbling knees, he got up, his face a mask of tears. He walked blindly to his room and collapsed on the bed. He knew he should not cry, he was a man, wasn't he? He was supposed to be brave, to be strong, and not shed a tear. At times, just like now, he hated himself. He hated that he could not stand up against his oppressor. He hated that he could not stop himself from crying, which she took delight in. He was weak, and for this, he despised himself.

A bitter laugh rang through the room. He hated himself as well, no wonder he was such an idiot. A failure. His mother was right. He would amount to no good. He could already see himself in the future. He would be an old man, alone, without a family. He was going to die alone as well, no one would even be able to remember his name. His grave would not be marked, and no one would be in attendance at his funeral. His fingers curled into a fist as he could not hold in the tears. He hated this miserable life of his. But what choice did he have?

IS THIS A SIGN?

George gasped as his body was overwhelmed with a sudden chill. He snapped his eyes open to see his mother standing before him, a bucket in her hand. He shivered from the cold water which she had just thrown at him.

Alessandra stood before him, satisfied that she had interrupted his sleep.

"Bum! Go fix my breakfast!" his mother said before turning around and leaving the room, shutting the door close with a loud bang.

George sighed as he rolled over on his now wet sheets. He looked at the time and groaned. It was just a few minutes after six, and although it seemed bright outside, it was too early.

"George! I don't want to call you again!" his mother yelled.

Sparing one last look at his bed, he staggered up. It seemed like it was a minute ago that he had closed his eyes, and now it was morning. A yawn escaped him and he stretched. He was very tired and it all had to do with his mother who had kept him awake for most of the night with her demands. He had been up on his feet running whatever errands she felt befitted him. And now, she didn't even allow him to rest, and he felt so tired.

His eyes were half closed as he prepared breakfast for her, making sure to prepare her coffee just the way she liked it. He carried the tray to the dining table where she sat with her nightgown, a bored look on her face. He stood before her as she reached for the plate. She cut off a little bit of the bread and munched on it. There was no anger, neither was there praise on her face. She reached for the cup of coffee and took a sip. George gasped, jumping in shock for the second time as she swiftly poured the contents on him.

"Is this how to make coffee? Don't you ever learn?" she yelled.

George stared at her, the now warm contents running down his face. He was pissed off, he wanted to yell at her, to tell her to stop, but he couldn't, the words remained stuck in his throat. Rather, he mumbled, "I'm sorry mom."

"Sorry indeed! Always full of excuses. You and that father of yours. You never own up to your responsibilities! Why I am not surprised? You look exactly just like him! Oh, God! He left me! How could he!"

Alessandra burst into tears and her body shook as she cried. George's heart wrenched to see her this way. When she cried, he always saw how fragile she was, and how much she really needed him. Beneath all of this, he believed she cared. With his soaking shirt, he reached for her, and she got lost in his embrace, sobbing on his chest as she called out for her husband.

He was not surprised when she pushed him away a few minutes later, glaring at him, and calling him names before she stormed out of the house.

At times, it was as if he had gotten his mother back, and it filled him with hope. She would laugh with him, ask him how things were faring, and even cook. However, her sparks were way more than her caring moments, and her kind moments rarely lasted. When she returned, he knew she would be cranky and mean, back to her normal self.

Today, he was off-duty at the grocery. It was a Wednesday, and he was glad for this because he could spend the day at the church. The church was a short walk from his home, and he made his way through the park to the church. He slipped into the back of the church for the morning mass which had started only a few minutes earlier.

His heart was heavy. It had been this way since Anton told him that he was leaving for Thessalonica. He had been thinking long and hard about his future. Most of his classmates from school seemed to be doing well for themselves. He saw their pictures on social media and they seemed to be having lots of fun, while he was stuck here. Some of them had even gotten married, and one had a child now. He was a man, twenty-one years old, but it still seemed like he was still a boy. He had no dreams of his, and he still lived with his mother who treated him harshly.

Would his life be this way forever? He wasn't an ambitious sort. He was content with the little he had, but how long would he live with such contention? He lived so comfortably in his misery. It pissed him, the way he was. What about those dreams he had had as a boy? What about those adventures he wanted to have? How he would run off, go climb a mountain, drive a car, and do something crazy. He had dreamt of traveling all around the world, having adventures, but all of it was no more. They were locked far away in a box he couldn't reach. Time had suppressed whatever dream he had yearned to come to reality. Was it time really which had done the damage? Or just him who was just too lazy and scared of the uncertainties out there?

His eyes drifted to his bag. The pamphlet he had gotten from Anton was sticking out of the bag. Australia. Wouldn't it be fun to go there? He had once had a pen pal when he was a kid in Australia. They had exchanged pictures and he always looked forward to going to the post office where he could get the mails from Australia. He had no idea where those mails and pictures were. Probably burnt or thrown away by his mother.

He let out a deep sigh as he rested on the pew. He closed his eyes, and whispered, "God, please guide me, I don't know what I should do."

When he opened his eyes, it was quiet. He looked around the church where he always felt comfortable. His mother was not here

31

screaming her lungs out while she looked at him with anger. Here, he felt at home, he felt like he truly mattered, and it always gave him a clear mind to think about his life, although the moment he stepped out of the church, he went right back to his original state.

He pulled out the pamphlet and looked at it, tracing the paper with his fingers. Australia seemed like it was at the end of the world. It seemed like some faraway country with monsters. He gulped as he thought of the horrible things that could happen to him in Australia. He could get kidnapped or labeled a terrorist. But then, what if it was bliss? What if he found the happiness he was looking for? He had never taken risks in his life, and looking at the state he was, it was no surprise. Perhaps, it was time for him to take a risk. All he needed was a sign from God, to show him that he was headed towards the right path.

"Australia. It is a nice place."

George looked up at Father Lazarus who was dressed in a black cassock. He got up and bowed before the man. "Father, good morning to you."

"Morning my child. How are you faring?"

"Very well Father," George said as he sat back on the pew.

The priest's eyes rested on the pamphlet. "Thinking of traveling?"

George let out a laugh. It now seemed ridiculous that he had even contemplated traveling. Who did he know in Australia? How was he going to fare? He wasn't qualified to do any white collar job or any menial work. It would be a miserable life out there. "Not really father," George said.

"You should go, it's a nice country, warm atmosphere, and warm people," the priest said. "It's not as if you're doing anything here. Your peers are spreading far, starting their families or furthering their education. You do not want to be left behind."

It was the first time the priest would say such words to him. Normally, he just asked about his well-being and work. It seemed the priest was also perturbed about his future, George thought with a grimace.

"It seems far," George excused.

"Is it not better to be far away? Where you can begin afresh? Start a new life?" the priest asked.

"But I wouldn't know what to do there, I don't have any educational qualification," George further excused.

"It doesn't matter. I'm sure you will figure it out. You're a bright lad. You don't really need some formal education. You could learn a trade. Or better still work with the church." A smile spread on the priest's face. "Now that I think of it, that's a great option. You have always shown an affinity for the church, right from when you were a little boy. You used to want to be a priest remember?"

George laughed heartily. That had been one of the several occupations he had wanted to be a part of, and he had been an altar boy in the church before he got pulled away by his mother.

"Do you remember Father James Nikkolopoulos?"

How could he forget him? When George had been about eight, the priest had been in his late thirties. George had been rather fond of the priest who made sure to give him sweets. He always made the sermons interesting and had been the head of the children's catechism class. He had always had a smile on his face, and whenever any of the children had problems, he talked to them personally, resolving their problems. George wondered if his life would have been the same after the divorce if the priest had been around. Perhaps not, as the priest was often known to go the extra length to make sure that the parishioners, especially the children were doing okay. However, the priest had moved away around the time of his parents' divorce.

"I see you do from the look on your face. Well, he's in Australia. He's now an Archbishop. An Archbishop, thanks to the Lord. He has asked of you a few times in the past, but my forgetful memory has always forgotten to pass his greetings to you. He's representing us very well over there and is truly respected by the Greek community of Australia. I doubt he will have any objection to you coming over. The Church can care for you, under his guidance until you find your feet. He has helped a few Greeks who went over there, and they attest to his gracious help. Problem solved George."

George was excited. This was the sign he had been waiting for. He had been filled with doubts, and just at the moment he needed it, God had sent the priest to him, affirming the decision he had been contemplating about.

"I think I will do it," George said with a shaking voice. He could not believe he was going to do it. He was going to leave his mother, his homeland, and head to a strange land. Did it scare him? Bloody yes! But the thought of it felt so damn good.

The priest smiled broadly, and let out a sigh of relief, obviously pleased that George had made up his mind. "I'm so proud of you. I assure you, this is the first step towards finding yourself. You won't regret a thing."

As he walked home, George was in a haze. Whew! He had made up his mind, and there was no backing out. The priest told him to return in two days, by then he would have reached out to the Archbishop and would have a response for him. The priest was however sure that the archbishop would be helpful.

He spotted the boots as he got into the house. His mother was home. The smile he had on his face vanished. Taking slow and careful strides, he walked into the living room, she wasn't in there. He could smell the aroma from the kitchen. It was one of the good days when she was able to prepare a meal, hopefully for both of them. When he walked into the kitchen, he saw her staring at the wall, the pot on the burner.

"Mama, how was your day?" he asked quietly.

She gave him a look. It was as if he was not standing right there, as she seemed to look through him.

"Mama?"

"I'm not deaf you idiot!" she snapped, glaring at him.

He took a step back, hurrying out of the kitchen before she chose to escalate her actions. This would not be for long, he told himself as he shut the door close. He was going to miss his mother, but he was certainly not going to miss her cruelty. This was for the best; he needed to get away from her claws. He needed to live.

AUSTRALIA HERE I COME!

"Mama, I am leaving."

Her eyes were trained on the TV as she ignored his presence, or soon departure. George sighed. Was she still going to act this way? Knowing that she would not see him for a long time? But then, what had he expected? After what had happened when he had first told her that he was leaving?

After he had met with the old priest, who confirmed that the Archbishop was excited to receive him with open arms, George had begun preparation for his trip with the meager savings hidden in his mattress that he used to get ready for the big trip. It was only after everything was done that he told his mother.

She had burst into a laugh, then looked up at him with tears in her eyes. "You're indeed a son of your father, aren't you? After all, I have done for you? After my sacrifices, you're leaving me for another woman? She must be a whore, isn't she? Taking what doesn't belong to her!"

As she edged towards him, he began to edge back, until he could feel his back hitting behind the wall. Her eyes were wild as she glared at him, barely any space between them. He gasped as her hands went to his face, her nails trying to scratch at him.

"Weak, just like your daddy," she whispered.

He had tried to reach for her hands, but she had done this so many times that she was experienced. She clawed at him anywhere she could, and in defeat, he covered his face from her sharp nails. Then she stopped. When he removed his hands from his face, he saw a sight which killed his heart. There were tears rolling down her eyes.

"Don't go, son, don't go, don't leave me," she cried.

He pulled her into his arms as she sobbed, filling his heart with despair. It hurt him to see her this way, broken. First, she had lost her husband, and now he was leaving. But he couldn't stay. Perhaps, subconsciously, he had gotten all his documents ready because he feared he would cave into her demands. He knew this softness in her would not last long. And when she turned bitter? He would be the recipient, and he would regret not going in the first place.

"I have to leave mother," he had whispered into her ears, hoping that she would understand why he couldn't stay. He worried about her being alone, but she could care for herself, and he would tell Mrs. Dolan as well as the neighbors to check on her. With his prayers, he was sure she would be fine. All he needed to worry about was himself.

He squealed when she pinched his nipple through his shirt, twisting the little nub with so much strength. He quickly pulled away from her as she hissed at him. He had been right on the mark. She had snapped back to her old self.

Now, as he stood before her, he knew she was not going to tell him goodbye. Perhaps, it was for her good that he was leaving. His presence might be causing more harm than good. If he was gone, she might change, become well, at least he prayed so. He leaned forward and placed a kiss on her forehead, then quickly pulled away before she could do something mean. He reached for his one luggage bag then went out the door, refusing to take a final look back at the house which had given him so many horrible memories.

Anton was waiting outside with his mother's truck. He was going to miss his friend as well, but he was glad that he was leaving; being here without Anton was going to be different.

Anton clapped him on the back. "I can't still believe you're leaving this hellhole. I figured you were going to live with your mama till you were ninety or something."

Both of them laughed, however, George knew it was a possibility if he remained in Greece. When he had told Anton of his intention to leave, Anton had refused to believe him until he showed him his traveling papers.

"Damn buddy, you shock the hell out of me. Are you serious?" Anton had asked.

George nodded in confirmation.

"You lucky bastard! You're going to leave the country before me. Make sure you have tons of girlfriends, I hear we're in high demand over there. You know we make the best lovers," Anton had teased.

The radio was on a low volume as they drove to the airport. Ironically, it was an old Greek song about leaving home for greener pastures. It was the perfect song to say goodbye to this mother's land.

"You sure you want to leave? You look like you want to stay back. I could take your place," Anton teased.

George smiled, rolling his eyes. He was very nervous. He had cooked up several possibilities of what could happen in Australia, and still, he didn't know what to expect.

"Don't worry, it's going to be alright. You will figure a way out. You always do."

George wished he was as confident as Anton. All he had on was a mask which hid his quavering self, which was his true self.

In about thirty minutes, they arrived at the airport, and they went through security. Standing in front of the boarding area, he turned to his friend who had been a huge support all these years.

"Plane leaves in a few minutes, I need to board," George said.

Anton grinned. "I'm not going to cry on you if that's what you want."

George laughed. He was surely going to miss Anton. He hugged his friend tightly, patting him on the back. "Take good care of yourself, keep the girls away, and be good."

"I'm always good, as for the girls, you know I can't promise you that. Have fun George, let it all go."

He gave his friend one last hug and turned around, walking towards departure as the flight was announced by a female voice over the speakers.

It was the first time he was boarding a plane and with the help of a hostess, he found his seat which was by the window. He looked around the airplane which was getting filled up with passengers. There were a few old people, but most of the passengers were young, some of them looking like businessmen. His neighbor was a lady who looked to be in her fifties. She mumbled a greeting, popped two pills into her mouth, and she was dead asleep before the plane even took to the air. All the better for him, the last thing he needed was to feel more anxious with personal questions from her.

There was no turning back now, George thought as the clouds quickly surrounded the plane. It all seemed like a dream, that he had made a decision, and regardless of the doubts, had gone through with this. Perhaps, he was becoming a man. That was the only explanation. He shut his eyes, getting lost in the dreams which of late had been returning.

*

It was afternoon the next day when the plane touched down in Australia. The flight had been smooth, with no altercations. As the hostess thanked them for boarding the airline, he removed his seatbelt, waiting for the stream of passengers to get down. When it was clear, he grabbed his overhead bag and walked out of the plane.

The first thing that greeted him was the hot air. It was a welcome to Australia. He followed the passengers into the arrival hall, and waited for his bag, before lifting it from the carousel. A smile was on his face as he made his way through the international airport, Sydney. He was here at last, and he couldn't wait to settle down. He felt like a child who had just been given a new book. He was excited to go through the book and make sure that he knew every word of it. Yes, he felt so much like a kid in this strange country.

Outside, there were taxis lined up to take passengers to their destinations. He looked around for the man he had been told would pick him up. He spotted him, a short man with a placard bearing his name, "George Margaritis." He walked towards him with the smile still on.

"You're George Margaritis?" the man asked.

George nodded. "Yes, I am."

"Identification please."

George showed him his passport and the man nodded. "Welcome to Australia," the man smiled. He took George's bag from him and led him to a black car with a white inscription on the sides, "Property of the Greek Orthodox Church."

George settled beside the driver, and as the car took off, his eyes were glued to the window. Australia was beautiful; there was no doubt about it. He had seen a lot of pictures in the past days but seeing all of it made it even more beautiful.

The roads were in perfect condition and there were no stumbling, or potholes, as it could be back at home. His eyes rested on the buildings they drove by. Australia seemed to be a cool place, at least on the surface. Getting tired of looking, he rested his back on the seat, tiredness taking over him. Being stuck in a plane, barely moving so as to not to disturb the woman beside him left him tired, with his body tight and sore. He couldn't wait to arrive at the rectory where he would get to stretch his body.

"How is Father... I mean the Archbishop?" George asked.

"He's doing great. He's a blessing to us. He's one of the best we have ever had at the cathedral. That man is so dear to us. All the parishioners love him. He always has his arms open, and a listening ear," the driver said.

George smiled fondly. It was exactly what he knew about the archbishop, he had not changed. He used to look forward to going to church because of the sermons of the then just father James, his words flowed like honey, and it made everything seem all so interesting.

"Is the church still far?" George asked.

The man laughed. "I heard everywhere seems far for you foreigners. Well, Australia is quite big. Remember we're a continent, and at the same time a country. Don't worry, we will be there soon."

Soon, turned into almost an hour, and it felt like George was taking another plane ride. Just as he was about complaining, or suggesting they stop for a bite, the driver took a turn in the road. There were now in a less commercial area, with the houses and shops looking friendlier. As they drove down the road, George could see the cathedral come into being. It was beautiful, and he held his breath as they got closer. It was the most beautiful church he had ever seen. It had towers and they were quite high, glistening under the sun as if they were shrouded with jewels.

The big gates opened and the car drove in, his eyes still staring in awe at the building. "It's beautiful," he could not help but say.

The driver nodded in agreement. "Yes it is, and it has the perfect leader, His Excellency, Bishop James."

The church was in the near distance, they took a quiet road which was flanked on both sides by trees. They soon drove into what seemed to be a little community, with cottages and rows of shops. One building stood out, a huge brown house which looked old, but had a rusty and homely appeal. The car stopped in front of the rectory.

"We're here," the driver announced.

"Thank you," George said.

The driver beside him, handling his bag, they walked up the stairs and rang the bell. It was opened by a tall, thin man, with glasses perched on his nose, as well as frown which adorned him.

"Jack, this is Mr. George, the Archbishop's guest," the driver introduced.

The butler's eyes rested on him, and he saw disapproval which surprised him. "I expected someone older," Jack said.

George laughed nervously. "I'm not that young," he said jokingly; however the frown didn't wipe off his face.

"Follow me," Jack said, turning around briskly.

"Ignore him," the driver whispered. "He's grumpy to everyone, including his wife."

This brought a smile to George' face. For a moment, he had thought the butler was not pleased to see him, not that he had done the man any wrong, after all, he was just seeing him for the first time. With another thank you mumbled to the driver, George took his bag from him and hurried after the butler.

The rectory was beautiful. It had a solemn look, but it just seemed to add more to its beauty. The interior was painted a dark brown, and peeping into the rooms as he followed the butler, dark furniture occupied the rectory. On the walls were several portraits of Archbishops and priests, who must have one time or the other served the church.

He stopped behind Jack who stood in front of a door, a bunch of keys in his hand. The door swung open, and George followed him in. The room was moderate size, and also had a solemn look like the rest of the house. There was a big bed with a canopy, a big chest, and a flat TV screen. There was another door which was open and led to a bathroom.

"This is your room," Jack said, shoving a key into George' hand.

"Is the Archbishop around? I would like to pay my greetings to him," George said.

Jack frowned. "The Archbishop will call for you when he needs you."

With that, the butler turned around, shutting the door behind him. George let out a breath and mumbled, "Spoilsport". He admonished himself not to be bothered about the man's rude behavior; the driver had, after all, said he was grumpy. With his dealings with his mother, he should know that some people were just that way.

He stretched his arms, reveling in the feeling and the loud cracks of his joints that filled the room. His room was perfect. Truth was, he had been expecting a less befitting room, one he would share with perhaps four others in a bunk, compared to his old room this one seemed like a palace. He walked towards the window and looked out. The view was into the garden which was filled with several flowers. It did need some work, and he couldn't wait to get his hands on a shear and rake. He was fortunate to be here and given such luxury. However, he needed to put himself to good use. He wasn't a lazy dude, and he would need to work to earn a living.

He would have to get a phone to call Anton and tell him that he had arrived safely. He even wanted to call his mother, although he had a feeling once she heard his voice, she would drop the call, but there was no harm in trying. At least, she would know that he had arrived safely and that he hadn't forgotten all about her, even if he wanted to.

He lay on the bed, and as he thought about all he was going to do, the tiredness overwhelmed him and his eyes closed, ushering him into sleep.

When George woke up, the room was a little bit dark. He looked at his watch and jerked off the bed. He had been asleep for almost five hours. He tidied up and left the room, deciding it was more than enough time to explore his surroundings and seek out his host. The rectory was indeed big, and as he looked around, the furniture looked quite old and exotic. They had to be really expensive, he concluded. He hoped he was not going to get lost because he didn't know his way around.

A door opened, and he was relieved to see another person. It was a slender woman with white hair which was cut short. She flashed him a smile. "You must be George. I'm Dorothy, you must have met my husband Jack."

Wow! She looked quite different from her husband who looked like a gargoyle. "Good evening, I'm sorry I overslept."

She waved a hand dismissively. "Don't worry about it, you must have been tired. You woke up just in time, the Archbishop sent for you to be awakened. Dinner is served and he would like to see you."

As he walked to the supper room with Dorothy, she asked him about his trip. He could not fathom such woman been married to Jack who had been hostile to him. He guessed opposites were attracted to each other, at least in their case.

She pushed open big doors, ushering him into the dining room. It was spectacular. The walls were high, going over to the next floor. There was a mural of the last supper painted on the ceiling, with golden chandeliers hanging overhead. A long table which was heavily covered with a thick tablecloth stretched from one side of the room to the other. On the walls were several pictures, both from the Bible, as well as the early history of the Church. The table was barely occupied, save for three men who from their black cassocks were priests. George's eyes rested on one man, Archbishop James Nikkolopoulos. Years seemed not to have wronged the man. He looked the same, only just a little bit older. He was handsome as before, his Greek decent showing in his pale blue eyes, and long black hair.

George mumbled a thank you to Dorothy and approached the Archbishop with happiness which was overwhelming. It was so good to see the man after so many years. How long had it been? He could not even recall. The Archbishop's eyes were trained on him as he walked towards him, it was as if the man was watching every step of him, taking every detail of him in.

"Your Grace," George said.

He was surprised when the archbishop pulled him in for a hug, patting him heartily. He felt so safe in the presence of the Archbishop. From the moment he had stepped into the rectory, he felt safe, most of his worries vanishing. The driver had been right; the Archbishop was truly one of a kind. He had that aura which made one felt at ease.

"George! You have grown a lot! I remember you running around in your pants, and now you're a man, a fully grown man," the Archbishop said, a teasing glint in his eyes.

George's face turned red, then he smiled as the Archbishop burst into laughter. "I truly appreciate your hospitality, Your Grace," George said. He had no idea where he would be staying if he had come to Australia on his own, or even to another country. The help the Archbishop was rendering him was going to go a long way.

"It's nothing son. Christ was kind to every single human, both to the Gentiles and the Jews, and to be Christ-like, you have to show kindness as well, to just about everyone, for we're created in the image and likeness of Christ. Let me introduce you to the priests, then we can have dinner. I heard you have not eaten since you arrived."

His stomach chose to rumble in agreement at that moment, making the Archbishop laugh, with George joining him. There were four other priests who sat beside the Archbishop. Father Maurice was a gaunt-looking man with tanned skin. He looked old, probably in his sixties, and he had a sharp eye which seemed to see into his soul. However, when he smiled, it transformed his face. George had a feeling he was going to like him. In a way, he reminded him of Father Lazarus. Father Maurice Gilbert was originally from London, he was small in stature, and was very friendly. He had a bubbly character, and as the Archbishop said, he was the life of the rectory with his British stories. Next was Father Isaac who looked very serious with glasses perched on his nose. He looked like a disciplinarian, and

George was told that he was more of a librarian, and attended to the church books. The last priest was Father Dante, who was just a little older than George. He was good-looking, and had the body of a surfer, with brown hair, and brown eyes. He had good looks, and George supposed he would give the female parishioners something to talk about. He was, however, the least welcoming, mumbling a welcome, with a glare trained on George. As he walked back to his seat with the Archbishop, he could swear that Dante was still staring at him with displeasure. That was so strange. He had never met the man, and he was directing towards him negative vibes.

The doors opened and there were a few more diners, there was Dorothy and her husband Jack. A slim blonde woman who was introduced as Amanda, she was the Archbishop's secretary and a host of others whose name George hoped he would remember in the coming days.

The Archbishop struck his silverware against his glass and the room became quiet. "Let's us pray," he said in a deep voice.

All heads were lowered and all eyes were closed as the Archbishop started the Lord's Prayer which was joined in by everyone else. Eyes opened and the dinner began. Dorothy whom he found out was the rectory's cook began to pass the bowls of food around, for everyone to serve themselves.

There were so many choices of food. Not even the rectory back in Greece had such luxury and he had thought they were pretty comfortable. If he was going to use the right word, it felt heavenly.

"So how's Greece," the Archbishop asked, who was sitting next to him, at the head of the table.

"I think it's the same as you left it. Nothing much has changed," George said.

The Archbishop chuckled. "I doubt it, you have grown up into a man? Haven't you?"

George's face turned red again. Him, a man? He believed he was a little more than a boy. Did he qualify to be a man yet? He doubted it. A man would cater for himself. A man would stand his ground when his mother raised his hand against him. No, he certainly was not a man. He had some growing up to do. Hopefully, the church would provide that opportunity.

"There's a lot we have to talk about," the Archbishop said. He frowned as he continued, "Father Lazarus told me a few things about you, and we need to talk about what you're going to do now that you're here. We have a lot of catching up to do George. Tomorrow we talk, but tonight just rest."

"Thank you," George said. He wondered what the priest had told the archbishop. Had he told him about his problems back home? He had never told the priest about the abuse, but there were times it seemed like the priest had known. Well, he would know all of that tomorrow.

"By noon, come to my office," the Archbishop added.

As the dinner continued, George ate quietly, joining in on the conversation when he was pulled into it. He was not a talker, and although he wanted a fresh start, he was beginning to think that that hadn't changed about him. He would rather remain quiet, taking all the information in.

The Archbishop was the first to leave the table, then the priests followed. George reached for his plate, with the motive to clear the table. Dorothy, however, stopped him, taking the plate away from him.

"But, I have to-"

She shook her head with refusal. "No son, that's my work. Now, unless Your Grace directs you to work in the kitchen which I strongly doubt, you have no place cleaning the tables. Go and have some rest, tomorrow might be a busy day for you."

George nodded, although he was unsure about this arrangement. He always did the dishes, and it was already a part of him. He reminded himself that things had changed, he would have to get used to the changes.

With Dorothy's help, he was able to find a phone to call home. Anton picked up on the first ring.

"Where have you been? I thought your plane had crashed, or you were kidnapped by a group of hot Australian girls," Anton teased.

George rolled his eyes. "I have been really tired. I am at the rectory now."

"And how is it?"

"Really good, it looks like a palace," George said.

Anton whistled. "Some luck buddy, if I was meant for the life of celibacy, I would be on the next plane there, but you know I love the ladies so much. Is there gold in there? You could take some and run back home."

George chuckled. It was only Anton that could think of such a possibility. When he was done checking up with his friend, he stared at the phone. Should he, or should he not? After a moment of contemplation, he called his mother. It rang for a while, and just as it was about to die down, it was answered.

There was silence. He was unsure of talking to her.

"Who is this?" Alessandra snapped.

"Mama, it's me, George. I have-"

He was not surprised when there was a dial tone. What had he been expecting? Her telling him that she missed him, and wanted him to return back home? He was however not going to give up on her, he was going to put her even more in his prayers. She would come around eventually, his faith believed in it.

He walked down the hall and bumped into Jack who had on a frown. "Why are you roaming the hallways?" Jack snapped.

George took a step back at the hostility of the man. He hadn't gotten the memo that walking around on his own free will, without causing any problem was a crime. "I'm looking for my room," George explained.

"Follow me," Jack said, before walking away without waiting for him.

His room was just around the corner, and he mumbled a thank you before going into the room. He had a feeling Jack still remained outside as if trying to guard the door or something. George shook his head in amusement. Did he think he was going to get up in the middle of the night and steal something, then run off? Jack certainly had some issue to deal with.

He lay on the bed with the lights off. The rectory seemed very quiet. It was a change from the environment he knew. A good change. There was no yelling at him, or a shoe was thrown his way. He closed his eyes and once again fell asleep, a smile on his face.

PLANS FOR THE FUTURE

The sound of the church bell woke George up. He lay on the bed, wondering where he was, and what was happening. Then, he heard a knock on the door. He staggered sleepily to the door. It was Dorothy, and she was well dressed.

"It's time for mass," she said.

It was only then he realized where he was. He was no longer home in Greece, he was now in Australia. He quickly changed from his nightwear and followed Dorothy and Jack in their car to the church.

He gasped as he stepped into the church, all feeling of sleeping now out the window. Inside the church was beyond spectacular. The ceilings rose high, forming a triangle which led to a point. The windows were all stained, scripted with images of the Holy Mother, Mary, and her son. Murals occupied every inch of the wall. There was one of Samson fighting the lion. There was Elijah on the chariot as he was taken to the heavens. There was also one of Christ as he fed the multitude with five loaves of bread and two fishes. Ahead, on the altar was the biggest cross he had ever seen, with the body of Christ nailed to it, tears of blood running down his eyes.

A divine feeling overwhelmed him. He had heard of such elevating feeling, but it had never happened to him. He felt at peace with himself. He felt like he could trample on snakes and scorpions and no harm would befall him. Still, in awe, he followed the couple, sitting beside them on a front pew. Soon, the pews behind them began to get filled. Although it was a Monday morning, there were a decent number of parishioners.

The sermon was quick but it was inspiring. Father Isaac talked about the need for love amongst all God's creatures. Men were all different, but regardless, we needed to love each other, just as Christ loved the church. George could not help but stare at the choir. They had the most sonorous voice he had ever heard. It felt like he was in heaven, as their voices lifted in unison.

When the sermon was over, he returned back to the rectory, still lost in thoughts. He was in an enlightened haze as he took his bath, getting ready for the day. Breakfast was served with just him as the Archbishop and priests had had their meals earlier on. As he ate, he thought of how he was going to spend the day. Explore the grounds as the Archbishop had suggested, then go for his appointment with him at noon.

He sought out Dorothy who was in the massive kitchen and informed her that he was taking a walk. The hot air greeted him when he stepped outside, reminding him that the rectory was well air-conditioned. He was glad that he had packed more of summer clothes, but he would still have to stock up on more, he had certainly not anticipated how hot it was going to be. Or perhaps, it was the difference in regions which made him feel it was that hot.

He took a walk to the back of the rectory. The garden was very large, and it led to farms. They were maintained, but he felt more could be done for them. He could imagine the roses blooming more beautiful, and the farms yielding a greater harvest. It was something he would talk to the Archbishop about.

Two hours later, George returned to the rectory. He had had an amazing time exploring the grounds. The church grounds were even larger than he had thought. There was a hospital, a shopping complex, and even a school, a sports center, as well as an orphanage. The church was contributing a lot to society. He headed to the kitchen for a glass of water but got a glass of lemonade in return which Dorothy gave to him.

"It's really hot here," he complained.

Dorothy smiled. "That's what you all say, but it's actually normal. You will get used to it. How was your walk?"

"Splendid. It's really beautiful here, and there are lots of amenities. It's like a small town. You don't even have to go out. You have everything you need in here," George said. He had not really had much expectation for where he was coming to; he had actually thought it would be a little church in some little town, but it was all mind-blowing.

Dorothy smiled even wider. "We thank the Lord for it. It wasn't always like this. The church was pretty small back then, but when the Archbishop came on board, everything changed. Then, he was just a priest, but he was very determined to make the church blossom. He has worked so hard over the past decade to make sure this church is what it is. We had about three hundred patrons then, but now, over a thousand."

George was very proud of the Archbishop. He had seen a cause and had pursued it, making sure it succeeded. More than ever, he knew he was in the right place. The good Lord had put the Archbishop in his path so he could learn a lot about life, and becoming successful.

At noon, George made his way to the Archbishop's office. It was in another wing of the rectory which was called the administrative area. It was here that the priests and the Archbishop had their offices, with other administrative staff of the church working here as well.

Amanda looked from her laptop when he walked in, after a knock. She flashed a smile at him. "George, you're just in time, please have a seat while I inform the Archbishop that you're here." She excused herself and went through a door. She returned a minute later and nodded, "The Archbishop is ready for you."

His heart raced as he approached the Archbishop's office. He had no idea why he was anxious, after all, the Archbishop was just a man. But then, was he really just a man with the respect given to him, and the position he had attained? Certainly not. He was a man, but a man of power.

The office was big, and well ventilated with several windows which were however shut close, the cool air from the air conditioners made the atmosphere cool that for the first time since he arrived, he felt a chill. The Archbishop sat behind a wooden oak desk which was covered with a couple of books and a tea flask. The Archbishop was well adorned with his amaranth red cassock, with black threading. The smile fixed on his face made George feel much less intimidated.

"George!" the Archbishop said getting up, walking towards him. He hugged him like he was seeing him for the first time, placing a kiss on his forehead. He led George towards a little circle of sofas.

"Your Excellency, I'm so grateful for your hospitality," George said. He knew he would never stop being grateful. The Archbishop had no idea of how great his hospitality was.

The Archbishop smiled amusingly. "You should stop thanking me, you're now sounding like a broken record. All men created by God are my brothers. Once I took my oath of priesthood, I swore to be kind to all men. Will you have something to eat? A drink?"

George shook his head. "No, Your Excellency, I believe I'm okay."

The Archbishop still insisted. He rang a little bell on the table beside him, and Amanda came in.

"Get the kid a drink, something cold," the Archbishop said.

"Yes, Your Excellency," Amanda said with a bow. She returned a few minutes later with a tray on which were a glass and a chilled bottle of juice.

There was a comfortable silence as they were left alone, George sipping gently from the glass.

"So how is the priest? Still kicking it?" the Archbishop asked.

George laughed. "I believe he's still doing so."

"Well, I have told him to retire, he has had some health issues in the past, and needs to rest," the Archbishop said.

This was news to George, the priest seemed as strong as a bull. But now that he thought of it, he no longer looked as strong as he used to be. Age had finally caught up with him.

"I must say, I was very surprised when he told me you were coming over. I have asked about you a couple of times in the past, but we never really talked about you. I figured by now that you would be in the university. I thought that by now you would become a doctor, a fireman, or even a priest."

George's face turned red. "You remember all those."

The Archbishop nodded. "I remember a lot. You were passionate about being all of them. Today you wanted to be a doctor, tomorrow an engineer, and another day a priest. So what happened?"

George looked away. "Life happened."

The Archbishop reached for his hand across the sofa and patted it. "Don't beat yourself over it. The priest told me he really didn't know much because you weren't talking, but he believed things at home weren't good."

George was quiet, the juice he had consumed itched to rise to his throat and get thrown up. Anxiety overwhelmed him and he felt so ashamed of what he had gone through. It wasn't a past he was proud of. He had not done anything wrong, but he had been treated so wrong, that he couldn't summon the courage to say a word.

"I apologize for intruding George, it is not my intention to hurt you, but I-"

"My mother was abusing me," George blurted.

There was no surprise on the Archbishop's eyes as if he already knew what had happened. George dismissed it, there was no way he could have known. The Archbishop was probably used to such tales.

"She would talk down on me, horrible words, and she would hit me. It got worse as I grew up, I reminded her a lot about my father who left her for another woman I guess. I think she's sick. She was not the mother I used to know," George continued.

"Tragedy tends to have a hold on people. Divorce is one of such. Can we really blame your mother for her ills? Yes, we can. She had an obligation to look after you her child. But then, as you suspect, she may be sick. In life, we have to go through phases, most of which are terrible. What matters is the way we rise from them. God doesn't give us problems we can't handle, and when it becomes too much to handle, he steps in and takes control. You're not here of your own doing, the good Lord has orchestrated this move from the time you were in your mother's womb. Sorrow may come at night, but joy cometh in the morning," the Archbishop said.

Tears began to flow down his eyes. He thought of everything that happened to him since his parents' divorce. He had gone through so much, and no one had known. There was so much pain in him, so much despair, and he just wanted to let it out. He was not ashamed as the tears began to increase, his body quivering as he wept for a childhood which was traumatized. It was as if he never had a childhood actually. Arms surrounded him, and he knew he ought to be ashamed for slobbering like a baby, but he leaned on the Archbishop, weeping.

"Its okay son, it will be okay. You're safe here. All will be well," the Archbishop whispered, caressing his hair.

George had no idea how long he remained in the Archbishop's arms weeping. When he realized how stupid he was to weep like a baby, he pulled away, his face tear-stained, but with no more tears coming from his eyes. "I'm sorry Your Excellency, I just... I just."

The Archbishop placed a finger over his lips with a kind smile. "Shhh... there's no need to be ashamed. I understand how you feel. I may not have gone through what you did, but life doesn't make you strong without experiences of your own. It will be fine son, the storm is over, and it is time for the sun to spread its rays all over your life."

He handed him a handkerchief and George cleaned his face, trying to compose himself. The Archbishop was right, that part of his life was over. He had left Greece, his mother, his father, and other forms of oppression behind. Here, he was going to begin afresh. He was going to start on a new slate.

"The rectory is your home, George. If you want anything, ask the staff, and if there's any problem, come to me, I will always be available to see you anytime. All you have to do is ask."

"Thank you, Archbishop," George said, he still found it hard to believe that he had had a change of luck. The storm was indeed over.

"I was told by the priest that you worked at a grocery and attended to the grounds of the church."

George nodded. "Yes, I would like to ask if I can attend to the grounds here. They are in good condition, but they still some care. I don't mind working with the gardener."

"Is that what you really want?"

George looked at the Archbishop confused. "Umm... I guess so. I just don't want to be a burden. I need to contribute."

"By being a gardener? Don't you want more?"

"I do! But... I have no qualification, I did not go to the university, I am not good with my hands either, well except for plants, so-"

The Archbishop shook his head in disagreement. "You're aiming too low son. You should be aiming for my position. That's what ambition is about. Let me tell you my plans for you. You're not going to work as a gardener in the church, old Peter is perfectly fine doing that. Nor, are you going to be the dishwasher. You're more than that George."

"So what am I going to be?"

The Archbishop smiled. "A priest my dear."

George' mouth dropped open. A priest? He looked at the Archbishop, hoping he was joking, and although he had on a smile, his eyes were serious. "A priest?" George asked nervously.

"Yes, weren't you passionate about being a priest when you were a boy?"

"Yes... but it was just a failed dream. I guess I grew from that dream," George defended.

"It's not too late to pursue the dream. It's the perfect thing to do. Serving in the house of Christ. The body of Christ needs you to help lead the lost souls to Christ. I know you're confused, you have lots of questions, but I have been praying about it ever since I got the call from the priest. The answer came to me yesterday when I saw you. The Lord wants you to become a priest. He wants you to serve him."

"Who am I to disobey him?" George asked in awe of the revelation of the archbishop. The Lord wanted him to serve as his representative? Who was he to refuse? He recalled the story of Jonah who had been called several times by Lord but had fled until he was caught by a whale. He could not ignore the calling of Christ; if he wanted him to be a priest, then he would be.

The Archbishop nodded in agreement. "We can't ignore the calling of God, he sees the future and knows what is best for us."

"How... how do I go about it?"

"The pastoral college, we have one here in the compound which you will attend. You meet the requirements, and I can help you if you want. You're chaste, aren't you? Never been with a woman?"

George' face turned red, but he nodded, and mumbled, "Indeed I am, Your Excellency."

There was a broad smile on the archbishop's face, which only made George even more embarrassed. "There's nothing to be shy about. It is good that you're chaste, men and women nowadays chose to involve themselves in sin. Being chaste is just one step in spiritual cleanliness. Don't worry George, you're in the right place. The school begins classes next week before then you will register. Living here, you will have lots of experience, as well as a recommendation, but you have to do well in your studies, and most of all, obey instructions."

"I can do that," George said, with conviction. He had failed before, failed to make himself proud, but this time around, he was going to make a good name and career out of himself. There was no turning back now.

MORTAL SINS

The night was cool; it seemed like a rain was approaching with how the trees blew with the wind. However, George knew it was just a show of strength, and that there would be no rain. In the months he had spent in Australia, he had come to understand the weather.

He climbed the stairs to the rectory and before he could tap on the ringer, it was opened by Jack. Even with time, the man was still not welcoming towards him. He took solace that he was not the only one who suffered the same. Perhaps, when he became a priest, the man would flash a smile at him, even if it was just once.

He made his way to his room and dropped his books. He had never been a fan of reading, but starting afresh, he promised himself to read so that he could pass the priesthood exams. He could not fail himself, he could not fail the Archbishop who he would always be grateful to.

It was three months since he had arrived at the rectory and so far, it was amazing. The Archbishop had helped him a lot, contributing towards him being a student at the pastoral school. His first week there, he had been quite unsure if the priesthood was really what he wanted, but recalling the vision of the Archbishop kept him going. He still had some doubts, but he knew that once he took the oath, whatever doubts he had would vanish. The class was relatively small, with about thirty other priests, most of whom were men born in Australia with Greek origins. At first, he had been quite shy to interact with them, but the church was a homely place, and he found that he fitted in, especially when they learned that he stayed at the rectory, under the hospitality of the well-respected Archbishop.

The theology classes were straightforward, there were no chemical equations to deal with, rather it was scriptures which he had been used to since he was a boy. The principles of Orthodoxy and how a priest should comport himself, he understood. He now had a clearer picture of what being a priest meant, as well as Theology. He was looking forward greatly to taking the oath.

With his education, he rarely had the time to think of the past. Being a priest meant you had to let go of your formal life. Old things were passed away. However, the past kept on creeping back, especially when he lazed about. He tried not to think of the pain caused by his mother, but it was impossible not to. It seemed the memories would never go away. He was learning how to forgive her as well, and accepting that he had not been responsible for her actions towards him.

He had called his mother a few times, and earlier on she had answered, hanging up on him, but whenever he called now, he got no response; she probably saw the long distance number and knew it was him. Anton was now at the university, and although they talked once in a while, it seemed like there was a strain between them, or it was probably just his imagination, or it had to do with Anton strongly disagreeing about him being a priest.

"Bullshit! What kind of fucked up vision is that? You know what? I had a vision too. You're not meant to be a priest! What are you thinking? Being a priest? I have been joking all this while and never thought for once that you will actually take it seriously," Anton had said angrily when George told him about his plans to become a priest.

"I'm sure about it. The Archbishop-"

"Screw the Archbishop. Think George. You want to throw your life away because that's exactly what you're doing. You don't want a wife and kids huh?"

George sighed as he thought of Anton reaction. He had tried to placate his friend that some denominations of priests could marry and have children, but Anton wasn't in support of him joining the priesthood.

"I just think you're making a mistake," Anton had said, before hanging up.

He still hadn't come around, but at least, he was still on speaking terms with George which he was grateful for.

As he headed for dinner, he bumped into Father Dante. The priest fixed him an annoyed gaze. "You should watch where you're going kid," the priest sneered, bumping into him before walking off.

George shook his head. He wanted to be annoyed, but was there really a need for it? He loved the rectory, he loved being under the guardianship of the Archbishop, but the only thing he did not like, was the hostility from the priest. He had no idea what he had done wrong to him. He had even tried to help him in any little way he could, but no matter what he did, the priest had his mindset against him. He rarely did it openly, but whenever they were together, the vibes were always strong. He tried to think back to the first day he arrived at the rectory, had he done anything wrong to upset him? No. He had noticed the priest anger towards him from the moment he saw him, it was as if he didn't want him there. George scolded him, he was probably reading too much into it, and if he was right, the priest would have to deal with it, he was definitely not going anywhere.

Dinner was without the presence of the Archbishop. He had traveled to Melbourne for a conference and would be away for a few days, he had left the running of the church to the most senior priest, Father Maurice. If George had thought that the Archbishop would forget about him, he was a hundred percent wrong. Aside from seeing him during mealtime every day, the Archbishop made sure they saw every week to talk about the progress he was making. George could not tell how he had found such grace before the Archbishop, but the Archbishop seemed to take him as his son. They spent evenings, or afternoons when both men were free from their busy schedules talking. With the Archbishop, he found a father, who listened attentively. He wished the Archbishop had been in his life when he had been a teenager, he was sure that he would have turned out different, and would have suffered none of the abuse, but when he thought of it, it was just the doing of the Lord to put the Archbishop in his path. Things were going to work according to when the time was right.

Dinner was a quiet event, at least for him. It seemed like the Archbishop's absence was a void which could not be filled. He froze when he felt a nudging at his feet. He looked from his plate to the person sitting beside him, Natasha. He sighed, not again. Natasha had joined the administrative staff of the rectory a month ago. She was a very pretty girl. She had a lean figure with curves in the right places with long black hair and beautiful eyes. There was a sexual aura about her, she knew it, and she used it to her advantage. George had seen her several times make a man speechless as she stared at him with those eyes of hers. Her eyes seemed to be set on him as her latest victim. She stalked him in the hallway, knocked on his door with flimsy excuses, and now, she had started the habit of trying to play footsie with him underneath the table. He knew the message she was passing across. He was not interested! Couldn't she read the message? He was being chased, and would not break his purity even though she was a pretty woman, and he should consider himself lucky that she was chasing after him.

He removed his leg from her reach and was breathing a sigh of relief when her hand touched him, just above his zipper. He was stunned, hitting his glass over. Luckily, the glass was empty.

"Are you okay?" Dorothy asked with concern.

"Yes, I am. I just... never mind," George said with a smile. He flashed a frown at Natasha who had on a serious face as if her hand had not just been on his lap.

With dinner over, he waited for the table to thin out. As Natasha left the table, he hurried after her into the hallway. She turned to him with a smile.

He glared at her with anger. He did not like the games she was playing. They were dangerous and he wanted no part of sexual iniquity. She was a temptation that he was not going to fall into.

"You need to stop this!" George snapped.

"Stop what?" Natasha asked, thrusting her body towards him.

He pushed her away, but she still pressed her body against him, a coy smile on her lips. "Stop this! I don't like this game you're playing Natasha, I'm a priest to be! An ordained priest!! I will have none of this. If you continue with this, I will have no other choice but to-"

Her lips met his. He was shocked for a nanosecond, then quickly pushed her against the wall. She yelped as her back hit the wall, glaring at him.

"Stop this!" George demanded harshly.

She rolled her eyes, edging towards him, her fingers trailing his chest. "You have no idea what you're missing, do you? You're a virgin aren't you?" Even in the dark, he could not hide the redness that overcame his face. He knew he was one of a kind. Most of the men who were in the theology school were not virgins themselves although they were spiritually chaste. It was rare to see a man who was a virgin his age. Natasha laughed, a gleam in her eyes. It seemed the thought of him being a virgin made her want him even more.

"I want to corrupt you, Father, I want you to punish me," she hissed into his ear.

A cough startled both of them, pulling them away from each other. George started with a pale face at Father Dante. There was a gleam in his eyes which sent chills all over George, with a smug smile on his lips.

"I will see you tomorrow George. Good night George, good night Father," George said, flashing a smile as she walked passed both men.

There was silence, one which riled George. He was angry at being caught in such an awkward situation with Natasha. Why on earth had she not listened when he had told her to let him be?

"Interesting," Father Dante murmured, loud enough for him to hear, which was probably his intention.

George was not going to let the priest have the upper hand, he may have caught them in a not so compromising position, but he would give no answers, he owed him nothing. He was going to act as nothing had ever happened; whatever the priest chose to believe was to his own peril.

"Good night Father," George said, walking towards the other direction.

"Good night George," the priest said.

George could swear there was a mocking tone in his voice, and that his eyes were firmly fixed on him. It was only when he was in his room, the door closed, with his back against it, that he let out a breath of relief. That had been a close call, he berated himself. What would have happened if Natasha had done something even more stupid, and the other priests, even the Archbishop had seen them? The last thing he wanted was to displease the Archbishop; he owed him far too much to do such a stupid thing. Natasha was strong headed, he had a feeling she would not stop until she had her way, which was impossible. He could not give in to her whims. He was scared, deeply scared about having sex which seemed ridiculous. He

66

had read a few books in the past and had once watched a porn video, but all it did was terrify him even more. He was naïve, how on earth was he going to go about it the right way?

He shook his head as he undressed. He should not be thinking about the mechanisms of sex. He was only allowing the antics of the devil slide through cracks of his holiness. He was not going to have sex, now or never. It sounded absurd, perhaps to others, but not to him. Others had done it before him, and they had not died, he was capable of doing it as well. He had not asked the Archbishop because it would not only be disrespectful but also uncomfortable, but he was sure the Archbishop was a chaste man who had never seen the nakedness of a woman. If he wanted to be like the Archbishop, then he needed to push away any form of temptation, no matter how alluring they seemed to him. He was going to have to wield an iron hand when it came to Natasha. He needed to get it clear to her that nothing could work out between them. There had to be men out there who would take just one look at her and want her in different ways possible. He was not that man, and he would never be.

The following days, he avoided Natasha as much as he could. Whenever he saw her coming down the hallway, he ducked. He made sure to get into the meal room late, so he could find a seat away from her disturbance. His plan was to put as much distance as he could from her. He knew deep down that the best thing was to confront her, but what had happened the last time he had done so? Besides, George wasn't one for confrontations, he always did well with fleeing, then facing the problem.

By the end of the week, the Archbishop had returned. It seemed the rectory had livened up with his return. He brought with him gifts for everyone; a few books and some clothes for George; the clothes were a perfect size, and he was glad that the Archbishop had chosen rightly.

That night, at dinner, however, the Archbishop was absentminded. Perhaps it was his imagination, but it seemed the Archbishop had his eyes trained on him more than before; it was as if there were anger and disappointment in his look. What had he done wrong? George wondered. And to top it all, he had arrived early for dinner, giving Natasha the opportunity to slip next to him. She was being careful this time around as she tried to touch him, but all it did was made him uncomfortable. It was as if the Archbishop could see what was happening under the table. He closed his eyes for a moment, and prayed, "God, please take this temptation away from me". When he opened his eyes, the Archbishop was staring right at him. He lifted his glass in greeting, and George lifted his back at him, as Natasha's hands crawled on him.

With dinner over, the Archbishop left first, the other priests following. George made his way quickly, hoping to avoid Natasha. He was however not quick enough, as he heard her voice calling softly to him. He tried to hurry his footsteps but she gripped his arm, pulling him back.

"Have you been avoiding me?" she asked hoarsely.

"Yes, I have! You need to stop!" George snapped. "This can't go on. I don't want you, Natasha. This is getting out of hand!"

"You poor baby," Natasha said, thrusting her boobs at him. He tried to push her away, but she had surprising strength, holding on to him, as she tried to plant a kiss on his lips.

"Stop this Natasha! Stop!" he said harshly, but not loudly.

"You know you want this, I want you too," Natasha said, as she began to grind herself against him.

The hairs on his arms rose as a shadow came into view. Natasha must have felt the presence as well because she drew away from him. He could feel his heart pounding as the Archbishop stood in front of them, his face blank, devoid of any emotion.

"Natasha, George," the Archbishop said quietly.

"Your Excellency," Natasha said, in a whisper.

"Go." It was just one word, said quietly, but it made Natasha hurry away, in what seemed to be a run.

"Your Excellency," George said with a quavering voice. Natasha had once again put him in a compromising state, and this time around, it was the Archbishop who had seen them. It seemed his luck had run out.

"Follow me," the Archbishop said, turning around.

His mind was filled with worry as he walked slowly behind the archbishop. What was going to happen now? He could explain to the Archbishop, but would he believe him? Natasha had had her body pressed against him, in the dark of all place. Would he lie to his Excellency that nothing had happened? That he had been trying to help Natasha? Would the Archbishop believe him, or see through his lie? He felt despair as he realized that everything he had achieved so far could be gone if the Archbishop had lost trust in him. He now understood why chastity was important for priests. Women were dangerous beings, and interacting with them sexually could lead to a man's downfall.

The Archbishop opened the door which led to an office, one he had in the living quarters. It was smaller than the other office. The Archbishop switched on the light, and the room was shrouded in bright fluorescent light.

"Sit," the Archbishop said.

George sat anxiously on a sofa, his hands on his knees. The suspense was killing him, making him want to blurt things out, but he told himself to remain calm. The Archbishop went to a shelf and poured for himself into a glass some whiskey from a decanter. It was the first time he would see the Archbishop drink, and it unnerved him.

"What is happening between you and Natasha?" the Archbishop asked as he settled down.

"Nothing Your Excellency. Nothing," George said.

"Really? What I walked into didn't seem like anything George. You may not have taken your oath of priesthood, but you are supposed to remain chaste. Are you trying to tell me that you're not ready for the journey ahead?"

"I am! I want to be a priest. I have nothing to do with this!" George defended.

"Then tell me what is happening. Let me understand," the Archbishop said comfortingly.

George didn't want to tell against Natasha, but he knew he had to if he wanted to be redeemed before the Archbishop. He had warned her, hadn't he? Besides, he had a feeling that if given the opportunity to explain what the Archbishop had walked into, Natasha would turn the whole situation around, making him out to be the villain. It was best he told the Archbishop the truth. Only the truth would set him free.

"Natasha has been making advances towards me," George said.

There was no surprise on the Archbishop's face as if he expected it. "I see," the archbishop merely said.

"But I never fell for it. Never!" George defeated.

"Tell me from the very beginning," the Archbishop said.

For the next twenty minutes, George told the Archbishop of all Natasha's advances towards him, and how he had tried to stop her at every turn, but yet she still kept pushing herself at him. As he spoke to the archbishop, he felt rage build in him. If only he had reined an iron hand, he would not be in this humiliating position. From now henceforth, he promised himself not to even as much as flash a smile to her, he was going to put her in her place. He was going to have no more of her antics.

"And that's all that happened before you saw us. Nothing else happened Your Excellency," George said, ending his story.

The Archbishop was quiet, then he took a sip from his drink, setting it back on the table beside him. He closed his eyes for a minute, then opened them, staring straight at George who was holding his breath in fear of what would happen. "I believe you," the Archbishop said.

George let out a sigh of relief. Those words meant a whole lot to him more than the Archbishop could ever imagine.

"I know where you're coming from son," the Archbishop continued. "Women like Natasha are very cunning beings. They are also weak beings who fall for the sins of the flesh. Remember Eve?"

George nodded. How could he forget the first woman created by God?

"She was so weak, that she fell for the lures of the serpent. He knew she was soft so he used her to get through to the stronger being, Adam. It is sad, but not all women are like our Holy Mother, Mary. I would like to blame it on the society. The mothers are not doing enough to train their daughters on the right path. Rather, they leave them to rot, all in the name of independence. Do you know what would have happened if Mary was the

71

first woman to be created?" He went on without George answering. "She would have been strong to resist the temptations of the serpent. She would have gone to her master and told him of what the devil had tried to do." The Archbishop chuckled. "We would still be in the Garden of Eden. Sadly, most of them are like Eve, entrenched in the sin of fornication. Evil, I tell you. Evil."

"Evil," George whispered in agreement.

"Yes. Evil. What else would you call a woman who knows you're chaste, and will soon take the oath of priesthood, yet she tries to throw herself at you? In the dark of all places? I'm proud that you resisted her. I am proud that you turned down her advances. Daughter of Delilah. They do not rest until they put their victims down to their knees, humiliated."

George' face lowered in shame. He was ashamed with himself for even entertaining her in the first place. He wondered if he would have given in if she had become more persistent, with no one finding out. He feared for the answer.

"Don't be sad son. You fought the temptation, telling the devil no. You're indeed ready for the journey ahead. You will face trials and tribulations for the church. But I can see that you're on the right path," the Archbishop said, a proud smile sliding on his face.

"Thank you so much, Your Excellency. I'm more than happy that you believe in me. I despise sin greatly, and want no part of it."

"Let us pray," the Archbishop said, closing his eyes.

George joined him, eyes closed.

TRAPPED IN HELL

Was it guilt he felt? Perhaps it was, but what option had he had other than telling the Archbishop about the happenings with Natasha? It was the following day after the incident, and Natasha was no longer at the rectory. Others didn't know why she had been sent out, but George knew. While the Archbishop was trying to protect him, he felt so bad for Natasha. But then, it was her penance for her sin.

There was a knock on the door and he wondered who it was. It was about nine in the night, and almost everyone had to be in bed. Standing outside was Father Dante in a long white nightdress, a displeased look on his face.

"The Archbishop wants to see you," he said.

"Is there any problem? Is he well?" George asked concerned.

"Don't ask me questions! He wants to see you."

Closing his door behind him, he followed the priest. He was filled with concerns about the Archbishop. Was he ill? What kind of call was this in the middle of the night? Ah. Perhaps he needed him to join him in prayers.

He had never been to the Archbishop's room since he arrived. It was on the topmost floor, far away from the rest of the rooms. They stopped in front of the door and the priest knocked on the door.

"Go in," the priest said, before walking away.

George walked into the room which was warm. There was a huge king-sized bed, whose posters were covered with inscription. Standing by a huge chest was the archbishop serving into glasses from a decanter. He was dressed in a white nightdress as well, and he looked less formal than he looked in the day. The smile on his face put George at ease.

73

"Come in, come in, don't just stand there," the Archbishop said. "Where's Dante?"

"He left. I don't think he likes me that much," George blurted.

The Archbishop laughed. "Poor Dante, I don't think he does, but he will come around."

The Archbishop walked over to him and handed him the glass, before walking off to the door. George stood, holding the glass, looking down at the content; he wasn't a drinker, seeing his mother wasted so many times made him forbid himself from drinking.

"Come and sit beside me," the archbishop said, patting beside him on the sofa. George walked over to him, settling beside the archbishop.

"Is anything wrong Your Excellency?" George asked.

"Would you have given into Natasha's lures if she had continued?"

George froze. He had not been expecting that question. "Umm... Umm..."

The Archbishop placed a finger over his lips. "You're curious aren't you? Of what it feels like? I saw it in your eyes."

George looked away, shame in his eyes. "I... I'm just curious, but I know it's all for the good of Christ. He would want me to be chaste."

"I think I was too harsh on you last night. You're a young man with needs, and you're not yet a priest. Men your age are sowing their wild oats. But you have to do it the right way, with someone who understands, someone who's chaste, not those who are descendants of Delilah."

George frowned in confusion. He had no idea what the Archbishop was saying. Was he giving him the go-ahead to have sex? Was this a test? Before he could contemplate any further, the Archbishop turned his head to him. George was frozen as the Archbishop's lips met his. His heart stopped to beat.

It was only as the tongue tried to prod into his mouth that he realized what was going on. He pushed the Archbishop away, standing up. There was disbelief in his eyes. He could not believe what was happening. He looked at the Archbishop in surprise.

"I…"

"Let me show you the pleasures, you need not sought outside," the Archbishop said, coming towards him.

"I can't! This is a sin!" George spat. This was a horrible sin before God, one which had caused the downfall of Sodom and Gomorrah, and the Archbishop participated in it? It made him want to puke.

"It's not a sin when it is done between two men of the faith. Is it with those daughters of Delilah that you rather lay with? Those unclean women?"

George flinched as the archbishop caressed his hair. "I have always liked you, George. You were one of my favorites when you were a little boy, but I never knew I would have such desires for you. The moment I laid my eyes on you, I knew you were God sent."

George glared at him. He felt so foolish. How could he not have read the Archbishop works of kindness? He was indeed naïve! "I can't have sex with you, Your Excellency, it is a sin. I don't even intend to have sex, not even with a woman let alone a man!"

"How do you know you won't enjoy it? Have you ever been with a man? I'm your Excellency, and I know what's best for you."

George pushed him away. He may not have had sex yet, but he doubted he was gay, and if he ever was, having sex with the Archbishop was something he would never do. "I'm disgusted in you. I thought you were helping me from the goodness of your heart, but now I know better. You're a fraud! I will forget that this incident ever happened but don't you ever again make advances towards me," George spat.

With rage, he headed towards the door. Suddenly, he yelped, as he was pushed hard against the door, firm hands holding on to him.

"You want to be stubborn? Do you want to resist me? Do you rather choose to lay with those dogs? I know you wanted her, didn't you?" the Archbishop sneered.

"Let me go! Let me go!" George struggled. The Archbishop, however, possessed surprising strength, pinning him down.

He felt his back being pushed against the bed. He tried to get up, but the Archbishop was on to him, pinning him down once again.

"You can have it the easy way son, or the hard way, you chose," the Archbishop said.

George looked up at the man he had trusted. There was so much meanness in his eyes that it scared him. "Please, I won't tell anyone, just let me go," George pleaded, he could feel tears forming in his eyes.

"The hard way then. Don't worry, I love it when others put up a fight."

George struggled as he felt the hands on his body, unbuttoning his clothes. He struggled even more as the fingers of the Archbishop trailed his now open shirt. He tried to jolt out of the bed, tears rolling down as his pajamas bottoms were lowered down.

"You can't do this! You can't!" George yelled.

The Archbishop chuckled overhead. "Yell all you can, no one will hear you. I will be the first to take you, over and over again. So pure aren't you? Get ready for me George."

George continued to struggle, the tears coming down like a flood. He cried out, but there was no one to hear him. For the first time in his life, he truly felt what pain was.

*

All around him was noise. There was laughter, and there was talking, but he could hear none of them. He could feel nothing. He was broken. He felt unclean, and no matter how much he had tried to scrub himself, it just couldn't go away.

He felt like a walking zombie, stuck in the timeframe of that horrible night. It played over and over in his head; he could hear his screams as the Archbishop drove into him, in a place forbidden, where he had never ever been touched apart from cleaning himself in the toilet. And yet, he had been violated, taken over and over again against his will. At a point, he had stopped crying. All he could feel was the pain, and hear the deep grunts of the Archbishop.

Monster. That was who he was. The man he had trusted so much, the man who knew of his horrible past had regardless of this facts raped him. He had thought the way his mother treated him was a pain, but he would pick that any day over what had been done to him. "But why do I have to suffer? What have I done to deserve this pain from the time I was born until now?" What he wanted to do was yell. Tell everyone what had happened. Shout at the Archbishop. Hurt him even worse than he had hurt him. But he was a bloody coward. He could not do anything, just as he had done nothing as he was raped, just as he had done nothing while being abused by his own mother.

He hated himself so bloody much. He hated himself for coming over here. He hated himself for wanting to be a priest, something which he now hated.

Why hadn't God helped him when he needed him the most? Why hadn't he sent angels to fight off the Archbishop? Why hadn't he saved him? He wanted to tell someone, but who could he tell? Everyone around worshipped the ground the archbishop walked. None of them would believe him. The Archbishop was a powerful man after all. Did he really want to tell people what had happened to him? Homosexuality wasn't frowned at anymore like it used to back in the days, people now were much more accepting, but in the church? It was still being frowned upon. Homosexuality was a sin before God, and he had partaken in it, whether or not he was a willing party to it. How would he tell people of the humiliating experience he had gone through? How would he tell them that he had seen hell, and was still lost in the embers? People that would not even believe him?

He was in a haze as he returned to the rectory. The once beautiful building now looked like a prison to him. He needed to get out of there. He had no idea where, but he couldn't stay. He could not live such a life of sin, and pretense.

"His Excellency wants to see you."

George looked up and realized that he was in the hallway. Amanda was standing next to him. He wanted to disobey. Yet, he hated himself for following her. He was such a coward.

He wanted to smack away the smile on the Archbishop's face as he walked in. Now, he could see the horns. Why hadn't he seen them sooner? Why were others not able to?

"How are you feeling?" the Archbishop asked when he settled down, the door firmly closed.

"How do you expect me to feel? You fucking raped me. Bastard!" George snapped.

The smug smile still remained on his face. "Now, now. You can't tell me you didn't enjoy it, because I did. I won't apologize for what happened. You will realize soon that I am only helping."

"You should be behind bars," George said quietly.

The Archbishop began to laugh, while tears started to form and started to come down the side of George's eyes. "Who's going to believe you?" the Archbishop asked at last. "With the time you have spent here, you should know how important I am. I did no wrong, that's what you need to accept. I'm saving you from these women. You're safe here. There's nothing you can do. You have your life ahead of you. You have my comfort, my protection."

"I don't want it anymore. I don't want any of this, you made me want to become a priest while all I wanted was to take care of the gardens! You tricked me! I want to leave!" George yelled.

The Archbishop smiled. "No one is stopping you."

He stormed out of the office, ignoring Amanda's concerned look. He went to his room and began to pack his things into his bag. He didn't care anymore. He didn't care if he was going to be a deadbeat until his last breath, as long as he was far away from the Archbishop, and his evil ways.

He opened his drawer to get his passport and travel documents. It was empty.

George' eyes widened. Where on earth were they? The realization hit him. He recalled the smugness of the Archbishop. He was not going anywhere. He slammed his fist against the table in rage. The bastard! He had nothing! He had no money to get another one because all his needs were catered for by the church. Not a single penny! Everything he needed to leave from this hell was gone!

He slid to the ground, tears rolling down his eyes, like a weeping child.

TEARS IN THE MIST

FATHER GEORGE
Eight months later

The piano hymn softly filled the room, as the line moved to the altar, the parishioners kneeling as they partook in the Lord's meal. It was a beautiful and solemn procession, with almost all minds set on the task before them, being in God's presence.

Father George was in full view of the procession, but his mind was absent although he seemed to have a smile for others, especially the parishioners. It had been this way since that very night. The night he would never forget. He was cold inside. He was empty inside. He was crying out, but no one heard. He was alone in despair, and it only drove him over the edge. The only thing keeping him was God, whom he believed gave him the strength.

The sermon over, he saw most of the parishioners off. He was the priest to a little church in Wollongong, a little town in Australia with just about a hundred parishioners. It was where the Archbishop had sent him, out of his sight, after he had used him. Discarded him like a used rag after raping him several times. After the first incident, George avoided the Archbishop; he sat away from him at the table, he made sure not to be with him when others were away, but the Archbishop had still been victorious, resorting to coming to his bedroom, and pinning him down as he raped him. One time, he had let Father Dante have his way with him. George would never forget the look of pleasure and spite on the younger priest who had always hated him. He had wanted no part of it. He didn't want anything the Archbishop had to offer. He had prayed and prayed, but he was doomed. He had had nowhere to go to. No finance. No passport either. Everything he had was allowed to the Archbishop. The only solace he had had was his priesthood. And after he had been ordained, the archbishop had tossed him far away, not wanting to see him anymore, not that he cared. He hated the man so much. He preached forgiveness, to love others as God loved the church, but all he felt for that man was hate, for all he had done to him. He had trusted him so much, believed him to be his saving grace, but he had been shown hell.

George was happy that he was away from the Archbishop. At least, it was an end to the turmoil, although he felt the pain every single day. However, he still was under the control of the Archbishop. He earned barely anything to go by, but what he did have, he was saving.

He took a walk around the grounds of the little church. It was a huge contrast compared to the cathedral. Here, the sun was hotter, the facilities barely manageable. It was like a punishment from the Archbishop to a man he had wronged. He yearned to do so much to the monster. To yell in his face. To hurt him. But he knew better, it was not going to be easy. That night, he had stopped being a boy. He had become a man. A broken man, but a man.

His living quarters were small as well, and he had a staff of three, who together doubled for other services. When he walked in, Matthew, his assistant was waiting with letters. He went through most of them; they were mostly bills for the church. The last however made his blood run cold. The seal was that of the Archbishop. He had ignored him for so long, or rather George had chosen to ignore him. Whenever there was a meeting, he never was there. He had gone at first when he had recently been ordained, but he could not trust himself anymore to not blow up when he saw the Archbishop smiling face, as he looked on with such innocence at others. If only the others knew how much of a monster their Archbishop was. But then, perhaps they knew. They had to know. They were all hypocrites, the bunch of them, and he could not stand them! So he refused to mingle with them.

He picked up the letter and went through it, his hands shaking. It was a personal invite to the cathedral. A mandatory invite which he ought to attend. In fury, he balled the paper up and tossed it into a corner. The nerve of the monster! How dare he summon him! After all, he had done.

The phone rang; he knew already who it was. The monster had called to make sure he had gotten the message. He shook his head at his assistant but Matthew was not the brightest of men, and as he had come to find out, he was a watching eye of the Archbishop who adored the Archbishop. The man thrust the phone into George's hand.

"The Archbishop," he mouthed.

George lifted the phone to his ear. He didn't say a word, nor did the Archbishop, yet he could hear his soft breaths. It brought back harsh memories, those grunt as the monster hurt him.

"George, my boy, it's been a long time," the Archbishop said, with a tinge of amusement.

"What can I help you with?" George said coldly.

The Archbishop chuckled. "Still touchy aren't you? You should learn to move past the rage, you will never get anywhere at such a pace. I thought I taught you better. I hope you will be making it over the weekend. There's a lot we need to catch up. Don't disappoint me."

George flung the phone to the wall. Matthew jerked in surprise, fear in his eyes. He stormed out of the room, racing the steps to his room. He fell to his bed, his eyes on the ceiling where a mold was. Tears fell from both corners of his eyes as he relieved the memories over and over again. Would they ever go away? Would he ever be able to look at himself in the mirror without seeing how tormented he was? He was no longer himself. He was dirty. He was broken without redemption.

He knew what the bastard was saying. He wanted to hurt him again, or perhaps torment him in one way or another. That was who he was. A master manipulator who had managed to have thousands of unsuspecting people look up to him.

His body began to shiver. He could see the smug smile on his face. His heart began to race as the panic attack overwhelmed him. His hands wrapped around himself, in a manner which he was used to. He closed his eyes, sleep not willing to arrive.

"I can't do this anymore," George said aloud to himself. Everywhere he looked to, there was a reminder of the Archbishop. He needed to leave, far away. He needed to heal himself. He truly wanted to serve Christ but he could not do this so in such a state. He could not do this when he had not healed. He knew exactly what to do.

*

The rectory was quite busy with several priests as visitors. George was in his old room, which he knew was a message being passed across. The last place he wanted to be was here, but he had a motive for it as well.

All through dinner, he was quiet, bile in his throat. The Archbishop had welcomed all the priests who had honored his invitation, and a banquet was been thrown for them. There was laughter all around him, but his eyes were empty. He hated the man even more. He hated how happy he looked. How unperturbed he looked. He was living his life the way he wanted, regardless of those he had hurt by the way. Father Dante was no longer at the rectory, the bastard had been cast away as well, and George felt no pity for him. In his place, there was a new priest who had written in his eyes eagerness to please the Archbishop. George pitied him greatly. He yearned to tell him to flee, but he knew his words would only be in vain.

"You're rather quiet Father George, they serve you better food at your parish?" the Archbishop asked, getting laughter from the other priests.

George ignored him. Dorothy's food was amazing, but he couldn't taste a thing. He flashed an apologetic smile at her, and she nodded as if understanding. He had become distant before he left, and he had wanted to tell all of them, but their loyalty was with the Archbishop.

He made it through the dinner gritting his teeth whenever the Archbishop talked. Couldn't he just shut his mouth forever? And why were the others holding on to the Archbishop's words with such respect?

"Welcome once again," the Archbishop said. His eyes rested on George as he spoke. "We have some catching up to do Father George, you have refused to come back home, and I wonder why. Tomorrow, we will have all day to ourselves."

George watched as he stood up. He looked like he was tired, but George knew that he was a fit man with a stronghold. He had learned this from his bitter experience.

He went straight to his room, but could not sleep. The room reminded him of that night, months ago when he had screamed, but no one had heard him. And he had been left bleeding and broken. He finally fell asleep and woke up about two hours later.

He stepped out of the room carefully, on tiptoes. The house was dead silent, but anyone could be awake, up to no good. Silently, his eyes alert, he walked down the hallway, pausing at intervals. He made his way to the administrative section of the building. He stopped by the Archbishop's door. He slipped from his pocket a skeleton key which he slid into the keyhole. He sighed in relief when the door opened. He made his way into the Archbishop's office, and the task began.

He worked in the darkness, putting on the light would set others off. He shone a torch as he looked around. Where on earth could his international passport be? He needed to leave the country immediately, without any further delay. He had made up his mind to do this the day he had received that invitation. No more could he stay here. He was merely wasting his time, as well as his life. Getting another passport was going to be bloody expensive, and he had a feeling the Archbishop would be aware of it and would foil his plans. It was best he found his passport and left. His bag was set, he now had enough money to book a flight, and go back to Greece. Far away from Australia and its painful memories.

He looked through the shelves but could not find his passport or anywhere his passport could be hidden.

Suddenly, the room was flooded with bright light. George froze, his heart racing. He had been found! He knew the fate that would befall him. No pleading could stop him! Slowly, he turned around. He didn't know if to be relieved or not. Standing in front of him was old Jack, a frown on his face. Both men stared at each other. Jack had never liked him, George was pretty sure the man would tell the Archbishop what he had seen.

"I-"

His eyes narrowed as Jack closed the door behind him. With few slow strides, he walked to the Archbishop's desk. He leaned lower to the desk and opened a false drawer. George' eyes widened as the old man tossed his passport and travel documents to him.

"How?" George asked in surprise.

Jack smiled sadly. "I am not blind or deaf to what happens in this house. I see things. Everything." He moved closer to George and patted him on the shoulder. "I'm sorry for what happened to you... but you know by now how powerful the Archbishop is. Sadly, more will come after you. You should leave as soon as you can. You never can tell what's up to his sleeves."

"Thank you," George whispered with appreciation.

He hurried back to his room, shaking his head. He didn't know if to be furious at Jack or not. So the man had known all this while! Why then hadn't he told him? He stopped himself. If the butler had told him such, would he have believed him, or rather told the Archbishop? He locked the door behind him and got ready his bag, shoving his papers into a pocket. At the first sign of dawn, he was leaving. It was time to leave the hellhole.

ONCE A FAILURE, ALWAYS A FAILURE

George looked all around. The welcoming smiles of the flight hostess and the airport employees were the first thing that greeted George immediately when he stepped down from the plane. It warmed him, welcoming him back to Greece. It had been a little over a year since he left Greece, but it seemed like forever with all he had gone through. One thing was sure, however, he was glad to be back.

It had taken him three days before he finally left Australia. Days he had used to settle his traveling papers while he lived in a cheap motel. He had left nothing behind, not a letter to the Archbishop nor to the parish. All of that was gone the moment he left Australia.

No one knew he was coming home. The only person he would have told was Anton, but it had been a very long time since he had last spoken with his friend. As a matter of fact, ever since the first incident, he had stopped talking with him. He had been too ashamed, too consumed with grief. So he had left things the way they were. He, however, missed his friend greatly. He envied him truly. If only he had gone off to school like him, his life would be much better. He probably had good grades, girls around him, as well as good friends.

He got into a taxi and gave the driver the address, settling down on the seat.

"Welcome home," the driver, a very tanned Greek man, with gap teeth said. "You lucky you left, got no idea why you returned, things not good here," the driver continued.

"Things are not better over there," George said quietly.

The driver, however, disagreed with his opinion went on to state reasons why George was lucky and shouldn't have returned. George didn't object to him. He had tasted both sides of the coin, and he knew he should never have left Greece. He was dressed in a simple Jeans and T-shirt, and all he had was one hand luggage, mostly filled with his cassocks and prayer materials. Although he hated the Archbishop and the church, he didn't despise God. He knew better than to blame the incidents on God. The Archbishop was just an asshole who was using the body of Christ for his evil deeds. Yet, he was not happy with God, for putting him through the tribulation which still had a hold of him. It was one of the reasons he had left Australia, he needed to find God again because he felt a void in his heart.

As they pulled into his childhood street, the homesickness began to hit him. He had missed home so much. It indeed seemed like a long time since he had last been here. He directed the car to stop in front of his home. He paid the driver and emerged. Nothing had changed much. The yard still looked as unkempt. He climbed the stairs and rang the bell, waiting anxiously.

The door swung open. Standing in front of him was his mother. She looked different, and he took a step back. She looked older, her hair disheveled, her face and eyes gaunt. She looked at him surprised.

"Antonio?" she asked.

George shook his head. Nothing had changed. "No mama, its George."

Her arms wrapped around him, and warm tears fell on him. "George! You're back. You left me!" she cried.

"I wish I didn't mama, I wish I didn't," George whispered. If he had known better, he would have stayed right at home and tried to work the whole situation out, instead of seeking for greener pastures which in turn ruined his life.

Inside the house was a mess. The living room had several bottles and reeked of alcohol. The room was also stale, and air needed to be let in. The kitchen had several plates overflowing in the sink, as well as cartons of rotten food. With his mother clutching to him, asking of his journey, he cleared the house up. He prepared a simple meal with the few items he could find in the house. A few minutes later, his mother was sleeping, her snores filling her room.

His room seemed smaller than the last time he had been in it. He chuckled without humor. To think that the last time he had been in the room, he had thought he would never return. He should have known better. Luck was not a friend of him, despair was. The room now seemed like a solace, and he wished he could take time back to the last time he had been here when he had been innocent. He closed his eyes and laid back on the bed.

What did he feel? Peace? Definitely not. He kept tossing back and forth on the bed. Yet, he could not sleep. Yet, there was still that emptiness in him. What had he expected? He quietly scolded himself. That he would fly to another continent and everything he had gone through would be erased? He slammed his fists on the pillow in rage. Nothing had changed. He was still broken. What he could do was try to heal himself. But how could one heal when every part of him was broken? Where would he even start from?

"What are you doing here?"

George' eyes flung wide open. Standing in front of him, with contempt in her eyes was his mother. He adjusted himself on the bed, his eyes still filled with sleep from the jetlag. "Mama," he said.

"Don't you dare mama me! I told you not to return! Didn't I tell you!" his mother yelled.

George let out a soft breath. Was this what he had returned to? He had hoped yesterday when she welcomed him wholeheartedly that she had healed. He had put her every day in his prayers, lighting a candle for her every night that the good Lord would help her. And yet, she was still the same. Did none of his prayers ever get answered?

"I... I had to come back," George said.

She glared at him, her hands on her waist. Then she cackled. "What did you expect? That you would become successful huh? You're just a failure. Just like your old man." She waved a finger at him. "Know that you're not welcome here. You better not think of eating my food, or staying here without rent. Bastard!"

She banged the door hard behind her as she stepped out of the room. He lay back on the bed. It was barely even morning. Would he ever have a peace of mind? He had run away from her and had run into a bigger mess, and now he was back home. His life was indeed messed up.

He couldn't sleep anymore. He got up, ready for the day. Before he stepped out of the house, he had to deal with his mother's antics. She was not happy to see him around, and before he could take a bite out of his meal, she snatched it and threw it into the bin, a confident smile on her face.

With a hungry stomach, he headed to the church. It had been so long since he had last spoken with Father Lazarus, and he admonished himself for it. Perhaps, if he had reached out to the priest, he would have been able to help him. He had felt all alone like no one could help him. The church felt gloomy as he arrived on the grounds, or perhaps it just had to do with his imagination.

He sat on the pews, his eyes opened. He felt no peace as he usually did. He had felt no peace in a long time. Would he ever be free, he wondered. Definitely not with what he had been through. How could he get rid of those memories? How could he stop remembering them? The thought of them sent a shiver all around his body, one which filled him with rage.

"Son."

He looked up and saw a strange face. He was not staring at Father Lazarus, but a younger priest, probably in his early fifties. There was a smile on his face, one which however didn't comfort George.

"I would like to speak with Father Lazarus," George said.

A frown replaced the smile. "You haven't heard?"

Dread suddenly filled George. "Heard what?"

"He passed away three months ago. He had a cardiac arrest right after evening mass."

George was weak. He reached for the hand of the pew and weakly lowered himself to the seat. The priest was dead? And he had not known! Oh, God! He hated himself so much. He should have been there for the funeral of a befitting priest who had loved and served God so much. Yet, he had had no idea. That bastard! He was sure Archbishop James had known but had kept the knowledge deliberately from him.

"I'm surprised you didn't know. His death was well publicized, and his funeral was indeed glorious. I'm Father Andrew, I head the parish now."

There was a call and Father Andrew looked back. "Excuse me," he said, before walking off to some parishioners.

It seemed like the walls were closing in on him. He felt himself choking. He got up in a rush and hurried out of the building. Father Lazarus was dead! He had been a man whom he had adored. A man who truly had served Christ. Why had the Lord taken such a good man? Why hadn't he taken someone like James? The world would be a better place then.

He had no idea how he spent the rest of the day, probably walking around in circles, thinking about his life. He had hoped that when he arrived back in Greece, he would meet with the priest and tell him everything, but now he was gone. How would life be for him now? Did he want to go back into priesthood? He truly did not know. He hated the priesthood, but he loved Christ.

Arriving home, he was greeted with shoes thrown at him. His mother was in a rage, her eyes filled with anger, her fingers pointing at him. "You rascal! Ungrateful rascal! You left me, after all, I did for you! George, why did you hurt me? Why?"

He tried to reach for her, but she pushed him to the ground. He groaned as he fell, narrowly missing his head knocking against the chairs. He tried to cover his face as she began to throw blows on him.

"Mama! Mama!" he shouted. Yet, she went on. With a groan, he pushed her gently away from him. She sat on the chair, breathing deeply with hate in her eyes.

Coming here had been a mistake, he decided. But where else had he had to go? He had nothing. No money in the bank. No work. No legacy. Nothing at all! The only place he had to call a home was here, where he was not welcome by his almost senile mother who had despised him for a long time.

The next couple of days were unbearable for George. He spent most of the time walking around and ending up at the beach, but it was hugely an eyesore. The school was out, and the beaches were a make-out session for anyone who was a couple. It irked him to see everyone so happy, yet he was on the outside, looking into so much happiness. He wondered if they could see the hurt in his eyes. If they could tell what had happened to him. He would if he saw himself, it was that obvious.

The moment he stepped back home after his wanderings, his mother launched her abuse on him. He could barely sleep at night because she banged on the door, telling him to get out. She was right, however. What had he expected returning home? That she would receive him with a warm embrace? That she would apologize for the wrong she had done to him? He had way too much faith in humans; it was what had caused him to be in the despair he was in the first place.

Two weeks after he returned, he went to the church. He needed to get a job. He was a priest notwithstanding that he had left Australia unannounced. He had been attending the masses, but truth be told, they were lacking greatly. Father Andrew was a materialistic priest, who valued the wealthy parishioners, instructing them to occupy the front rows, while the poor, the back rows. The wealthy new to this, reveled in it, blessing the priest with whatever he needed. He had watched from the pews the discrimination, one Father Lazarus would never have allowed. Yet, he wanted a job, and this seemed like the only one he could get.

"Why did you leave Australia?" Father Andrew asked, non-interest written all over his face.

"I needed to get away, everything there was overwhelming," George said.

The priest quirked a brow. "Not what I heard from the Archbishop, he had a nasty report about you."

"He's wrong," George said. He should have known that the Archbishop would come after him. Had he really expected to go scot free?

"I can't take you in here."

"I can attend to the grounds, I used to do it while Father Lazarus was here," George said. All he needed was something to give him some income, no matter how little.

The priest pinned him with a hostile gaze. "There's nothing here for you."

By the end of the day, with his credentials, George had visited about three other parishes, but none had been willing to open their arms to him, not even for a menial job. What had happened to the church of Christ? Couldn't they see that he needed help? Couldn't they see that his heart was heavy? The next days, he sought a job without his priesthood capacity, just as a common man, but he was turned back every time. There was no love anymore. No one was willing to even give him a piece of bread. He went home tired, broken once again.

He was tired of it all. Of the horrible life, he had lived. He was tired of the trust he had had in man which had been broken. The rain poured down on him and his white shirt, and black trousers, as he walked home, not a penny in his pocket. His legs gave way and he went on his knees, his tears submerging with the rain.

"Why me Christ! Why me!" George cried, his eyes looking up to the heavens, his fingers in fists.

He knelt there weeping, begging for Christ to ease the pain, but all it seemed to do was overwhelm him. He asked for a miracle, for help with the travails he was going through, but the only response he got was a car driving past him, and splashing him with muddy water. George went home with a plan. He headed, his body covered with mud to his mother's drug cabinet. He grabbed a bottle of pills and went to his room.

His body shivered as he wrote down a letter. It contained everything he had gone through in his short life. From his mother's torment to him leaving the country, and his return. As he read the words to himself, he began to cry. Seeing his life in the words could not even tell the misfortune he had been through. He opened a random jar of pills and popped every single one of them into his mouth.

He lay on the bed, breathing softly, as he waited for his fate. "Now I die," he whispered. In death, he would find answers to why his life was filled with misfortune. In death, he would find the peace he needed. As a priest, he knew the repercussion of what he was doing. He would not go to heaven, for that he was sure. He cried out as his stomach began to burn, the searing pain leading to his head. He closed his eyes, willing for death to overtake him. Yet, even death considered himself too unfortunate to grace his embrace. All he encountered was a raging headache and a runny stomach.

He woke up the next day, weak from flushing out his intestines, as well as an empty stomach. Other than that, he was still alive and could hear his mother yelling obscenities at the TV in the living room. He looked like a mess in the bathroom's mirror. His eyes were bloodshot, and his beard was almost covering his mouth. He looked like he had spent the last days in the dumps. Why had he not just died? He asked no one in particular. What mission did he have here on earth? Why was God being cruel to him, instead of reliving him of his pain?

"I saw your friend yesterday," Alessandra's voice stopped him as he fried some bacon in the pan.

"Who?" George asked quietly.

"Sal. He has a car now. He said he's a doctor. He looked very responsible. He asked about you," Alessandra said.

Perhaps, this was one of her good days, George hoped. "And what did you tell him about me?" George asked. He had hoped not to see any of

96

his schoolmates. Most of them had to be doing well for themselves. The other day, at the beach, he had seen Chris, who had been quite a terror back then, but he had looked in great shape, a wife with him, and two little kids. He had hidden behind the trees. What could he tell his friends when he met with them? That he had had the opportunity to go to Australia and had returned with nothing? They had always thought lowly of him, just another reason to add to it.

His mother's laughter sent a chill through him. He knew at that moment that today was one of the many days. "I told him the truth. That you're a rascal who can't take care of himself. That you still live with your mama, and all you do is eat my food!"

"I'm trying!" George turned around yelling. "Do you think it's easy for me? Do you really think that?"

His mother was stunned for a moment. She had never heard him yell. She recouped quickly and glared at him. "Why am I not surprised that you're yelling at me? You think you have grown some wings huh? Didn't I tell him the truth? That you're a failure? I have always told you! That's all you will ever be!" She began to clap her hands in excitement, chanting, "Failure! Failure!"

George tried to drone her out, but her words continued to haunt him. She was right. He was a failure. And it was all he would ever be. It was time to accept his true calling. He headed to his room and grabbed his duffel bag. It contained all he had in life. As he walked away from the house, his mother's chant continued to follow him.

BEING HOMELESS

The bread and juice were quickly munched down by George. It was the most he had had in days now. He would have liked to save some for later, but there really was nothing to save as regards the tiny meal. He eyed the line of people who were waiting for their turn of the free food given out by the charity organization. He looked down at his palm which had been stamped to show he had been given food. He sighed. Couldn't they just give him another round of food? But then, everyone probably wanted the same.

As a new set of people settled on the table, he got up, lifting the bag over his shoulders. He saw the look of disgust on their faces as he walked away. As if they were better, he thought annoyingly. But he supposed they were better. They weren't dressed in clothes which were almost rags like him. They didn't have long hair and beard which could serve as a bird's nest. They weren't homeless like him. They were hungry, but they probably had some place to rest their head, and take a shower.

Nowadays, he didn't bother to check himself on the windows. He knew how he looked. He was a homeless man who wore the same clothes for days, only changing his clothes when he had some money to pay for some time at a public bathroom to wash his clothes. Those days were however rare. The beach, however, was always the place he went to clean up. He did so in the night when the cruel looks of disgust couldn't get to him. It was there he took his bath, washed his clothes, and slept under the trees. It was either that or between alleys. Wherever he found himself.

George had lost count of how long he had been living on the streets. Five months? Seven months? A year? He really couldn't tell. He didn't even bother. What was the need? The day he had left his mother's house, he had since not returned. He was crazy already, staying there with nothing to do and without even a little bit of love would only drive him over the edge. For his sanity, perhaps also for his mother who had gotten worse, he had to leave. The only place he had known to go had been a shelter. It had been a horrible experience for him. The first night there, his bag had been stolen. It had contained nothing valuable except for his cassocks, rosary, crucifix, documents, and a few clothes, yet the thief had taken it all. It had been his first introduction to the harsh realities of life on the streets.

What had followed had been worse. He had been thrown out of the shelter on the third day with nowhere else to go to, the other shelters either filled up or not willing to accept anyone. He had had no option than to take to the streets, taking food from the bins as he saw others do, and sleeping in cardboard. It was a huge humiliation. He had been hungry before but had never resulted in digging out food from bins. However, he needed to what he could to keep on surviving. Whenever there was a soup kitchen in the area, he was always there, ready to take whatever good meal he could get. On a good day, a stranger could put some money into his hand, and that could keep him going.

It was a difficult life. He had never been on a high pedestal, but he had indeed fallen to the lowest rung that he now found himself. Barely anyone was willing to help. This he had realized earlier on. He had thought the church would open their doors to him in this state, let him sleep on the pews, or do some work, but one look at him, and they drove him out, shouting at him to never come back. What had happened to the house of Christ? What had happened to love and kindness? The principles Christ had come to teach? That he had sacrificed his life for? All they did was scorn him, look at him with dismay, and laugh. Only a few stopped to lend a hand, and all he could do was bless them in those words which would never depart from his mouth.

At times, he sat, his back against the wall and laughed. How his life had turned out. Should he have instead remained in Australia, under the abuse of the Archbishop? Wouldn't that have been a better fate than the state he was in? A priest now turned homeless. Then, he would curse himself out. How in Christ's name would he choose such a life of abuse?

One that he was treated like an animal by a man who called himself a child of God? He would rather remain on the streets, than in the luxury of such a cruel man.

In addition to the lack of luxury on the streets, there came the life of crime. It was tough out there, with the gangs, the thefts, and the mobs. He made sure to scout the area every night before he slept. Only on a few occasions had he been privy to a life of crime, choosing to turn to the other side when he saw them carry out their activities. What other option did he have? Preach to them? He was unlucky, he was all alone, but he was not foolish. His life was miserable and he had no reason why he was living, but it was better he still had his life at the end of the day.

He walked into an alley and sat by some crates. This was usually his spot in the city. He could hear the traffic as people rushed home for the evening. Soon, it was dark and he lay on the crates, the noise in the distant, as the nightlife took over. His back was uncomfortable against the hard surface of the crates which he had arranged as a table. He adjusted several times, but he knew he would never find a comfortable side to lie on. It was best to manage it till morning.

His head throbbed from walking all day, but he had no money to purchase aspirin for the headache. He barely had any cash with him. He went out every day to look for a job, but there was barely anything the employment sector had to offer him. Mostly, he did menial jobs; he cleaned, he acted as a building laborer and a gardener whenever there was an opening. However, one look at his face, and his inability to provide a referee, and employers were always hostile. Whenever he found a job, although he earned stipends, the treatment that was melted down to him was devastating. His employers treated not only him but others like him as if they were animals. All because they were so poor that they had nothing to rely on than such lowly jobs. They would yell obscenities at them, and at

100

times, refuse to pay them for their services, threatening to call the police if they didn't leave.

The world was such a horrible place, starting from the church. Where was love? Everyone was just so preoccupied with their selfish interests rather than helping their fellow man seemed like a great task. Although he had little, he tried to share with others that had even less, like other homeless people had done with him in the past. If he saw someone who was in greater need, a pregnant woman, a disabled, a drug addict, he was always willing to render help, even if it was with just a piece of bread that he had. There were times he had left a shelter because he had given up his space for someone who seemed to have a greater need. He knew how it was to be without help, and notwithstanding his inconvenience, he was going to help them.

The night was one of such, where he lay awake tossing, his eyes to the sky. As it got further into the night, the night got quieter, yet he could not sleep. So many thoughts filled his mind. He missed comfort a lot, a soft bed, warm blankets, and a well-cooked meal. He missed a decent bath, and he missed good clothes, but that ship had long sailed. He had no idea how long he would be stuck in this life. Years? Until his death? He had seen men older than him who were homeless, murmuring to themselves as they picked from the bins. He worried as he saw himself in these men. Just because he lived a clean life on the streets didn't mean he could not die on the streets. He didn't do drugs as he saw most of the men and women on the street do. He had been approached some time ago by some kids to help them sell drugs because he was an unsuspecting fellow, but instead, he had preached to them. Drugs were horrible. He saw people on the streets take the horrible substances, and they were no longer themselves. Too many were found dead in the corner of the street, a needle in their arm. Yet, he envied them. They were in a world of their own. They couldn't tell the reality of life. They couldn't feel the pain he felt every single day. There were, however, several more things he could die from. From a drunk driver. From a robbery, or a gang fight. From cold. From food poisoning. And most of all, from being broken.

He closed his eyes, and they quickly snapped open. His body began to shake, and it was definitely not from drugs. All he could see were those blue eyes filled with sick desire, as they pinned him down on the bed. He could hear the grunts as he was hurt over and over again.

"Stop! Stop it!" George began to cry. Yet, he couldn't stop the pain that had happened to him, and he was still reliving. Tears began to roll down his eyes as he lay there in the middle of the night. They would never go away. No matter how much he prayed or tried to shut them out, he would still continue having the nightmares, and attacks. They were what kept him awake at night and freezing at a spot in the day. He wished he could stop to remember. He wished he could forget. But life had cursed him to remember every single detail, down to the time it had happened over the seven months he had spent in Australia. Some called it PTSD, he had no words for the trauma he went through every day. He couldn't function as a normal person. No matter how much he tried to scrub himself, he remained unclean.

Although physical damage had not been done to him, he felt that everyone could see what had happened to him. A part of him had been stolen, and he would never be whole again. He was messed up in every way possible, and it was a wonder that he was even alive. Would it not be better if he was dead? He had no idea why Christ was still keeping him alive. He should have let him die out in the cold. Or get hit and left bleeding by a car. Yet, he kept him, dragging on his lifespan, using him as a puppet. It was in the early hours of the morning, he finally closed his eyes, falling into a sleep marred by monsters with blue eyes.

A SURPRISE MEETING
One year later

The laughter drifted to him and he scowled. The beach had become his home, and he hated when it was being occupied by others, especially the kids. They were always restless. Running about. Playing. And shouting. As well as littering the beach with all sorts of dirt. Their parents never cautioned them, letting go of them to do whatever they wanted. And when he scolded the children? They would yell at him, call him a madman, and even throw sand at him. He definitely looked like a madman with the beards which covered his mouth, and his hair which was almost covering his eyes. Nowadays, he just minded his business, the same way the world and Christ-minded theirs. Everyone kept to their own self. Perhaps, the world was better this way.

He lay under a tree, his bag under his head, serving as a pillow. It was early in the morning, and the beach was beginning to get filled with adults and children who would rather not stay in their homes. He would have to get up and take care of himself, then find some food, and be out of the way before the patrols would find. They usually ignored him, but at times, they would yell to him to go away.

An hour or so later, he sat under the same tree, his eyes looking everywhere but seeing nothing. He didn't wander anymore, just going around the places he knew in circles. There was nothing out there for him, he had come to realize it. He had hoped in the early months that the Lord's grace would find him. That some way, he would get out of this life, but nothing had changed, and he knew nothing would. This was how he would live till he took his last breath. He was angry at himself, for willing to accept his fate, but what could he really do? How could he survive without having anything to his name? Even the church that he had always trusted had forsaken him, and so had Christ. If others, especially his Creator had abandoned him, what other option did he have than to wait for his final moment on earth, after which he could ask the Creator questions why he had been made unfortunate.

He tried to zone out the chatter around him, but it was never possible. He wondered how people could be this happy with all the ills going on in the world. He could not even remember if he had been happy as a child. He doubted it. Yet, here they were, all happy with their parents, not a care in the world. He closed his eyes and opened them. He wished it was nighttime, his favorite and worst time of the day. Favorite, because it was quiet, with few souls to disturb him. Worse, because then the nightmares came. Whoever had said time heals all wounds was a bloody liar. Time only worsened the pain; it only made the pain more etched in his mind, and in his soul. Seeing how weak he was, thinking over the situation over and over, and how he could have averted it, wishing he could turn back the hands of time, and thinking of ways to hurt his oppressor only filled him with more pain. The wound was still open, and he doubted it would ever heal.

Forgiveness was important. He had heard this several times as a priest and had preached it to others, but he could not forgive James Nikkolopoulos. Not after the man had taken everything from him. There was no room for forgiveness for him. And if it was the only thing holding him back from moving on, he didn't mind being held back. The Archbishop didn't deserve to be forgiven. Men like him lived their life doing whatever they wanted because they knew no one would prosecute them. It was that smugness he despised, that confidence he hated. Men like him ought to suffer for their sins and rid the world of such evil.

His eyes focused on a spot in the water. There was something there, probably a ball lost from the kids playing around. Before he could move his eyes, he saw it better; hands, waving for help. Everyone was so preoccupied that they couldn't see the child drowning, not even the careless parents. He turned away. Did it matter if some child died in the water? It wouldn't be the first time. Death happened every day. Perhaps, what the family really

104

needed was a death to soil their happiness, just as his happiness had been destroyed as a child. At least, it would keep the families away for some time, and they would begin to look out for each other more.

Yet, he found himself jumping to his feet, hurrying towards the water. A life was important, regardless of life being a failure. The child was drifting away when he jumped into the water, the little hands sliding underneath the water. The tides were high, but staying on the beach had made him an experienced swimmer. He made his way into the water, looking out for the child.

He found the little boy, his eyes closed, and his hands weak. He swam to him, and pulled him up, making his way to the surface of the water. As he carried the boy to the shore, a crowd had begun to form. At last, he thought with annoyance. Now, they had their senses in check, which would go away when he turned his back on them.

A familiar looking woman pushed through the crowd and hurried to him as he laid the boy on the sand.

"James!" she cried, clutching the boy. "James!"

The boy wasn't that little, George realized, probably in his mid-teens, however, he had a small stature. Her lips met the boy and she began to send him some oxygen with her breath. He sighed with relief as the boy jerked, water pouring from his mouth as the boy's eyes flung open.

The crowd had begun to disperse as they realized that the boy was alive and that there was no story to tell. Of course, he thought with an eye roll. Heading towards them were medics, with a stretcher.

"James!"

He turned towards a man, running towards them, the cones of ice-cream he had had, now on the sand.

"This man saved him! He saved our James!" the woman cried as she hugged the man, the medics lifting James on to the stretcher.

It was his cue to leave. He didn't want the attention. He didn't want any disturbance from anyone. He had done his part and needed to blend back into his position. Besides, he didn't feel comfortable. Perhaps, it was the show of emotion, but there was just something too familiar about the family, especially the father. His blood raced to get out of there as soon as possible.

As he turned to leave, a hand was placed on his shoulders. He froze, his heart racing. Why he had no idea.

"Thank you so much, I can never repay you for saving my son," the voice said.

George knew that voice. He would recognize it anywhere, even in his sleep, even after more than a decade since he had last heard it. It was that of his father's. He froze, unable to believe it. How crazy the odds were. Then he was filled with anger. He cared for the life of a son and despised the life of another. He didn't want to be a part of this charade, but he needed to confront the man who had been a party to the detriment of his life. He turned around, and every doubt was gone, he was staring right into eyes which were as black as his. The man he was looking at was an older version of himself, amidst the beards, and unkempt look.

The man stepped back in shock. His eyes narrowed as he looked at his son's savior. Then his eyes widened as he took the man in. "George!" he croaked in disbelief.

George was surprised that he could remember him. But then, they looked so similar, a bone of contention his mother had greatly disliked. He began to hurry away. He could not do it. Stay around a man who he despised so much for abandoning him. He could hear the man call after him, and he began to hurry even more. He went under the tree and grabbed his bag.

"George!" the voice called, getting closer and sounding out of breath.

George began to run. He needed to get away as far as possible. He could feel the walls caving in. An attack on the way. He could hear the footsteps hurrying behind him, and he began to hurry as well. He felt the hand reach for him, but he ran into the busy road. He just needed to get away.

Suddenly, he heard a screeching sound, and everything went dark.

*

It was too bright all around him. It was like he was in the clouds, floating. He closed his eyes, and it was quiet, except for a ringing headache which overwhelmed him.

When he woke up again, he felt much better. His eyes adjusted to his surrounding and he realized he was in the hospital. He laughed bitterly, the only time in a long while that he had a comfortable bed underneath him, and it had to be in a hospital.

He tried to get up from the bed, but he felt a jolt of pain, and he settled back on the bed. Memories began to float in his head. He glared at the wall as he thought of the last thing that had happened before he was hit by a vehicle. His bloody father had been chasing after him. How great to have seen him, and end up in the hospital. The man would just never stop ruining his life.

The door opened and he glared at his father stepped into the room, followed by a nurse. The nurse smiled at him, but he growled at her, not cracking her cheerful mood.

"Good afternoon Mr. George. We are all glad that you're awake," she said.

"How long have I been out?" George asked.

"Over twenty-four hours. Thankfully, not much damage was done by the vehicle which ran you over. You have a few bruises but that's all. You should be back in shape in no time," the cheerful nurse continued. "I will be back with the doctor to check up on you."

There was silence when the door closed behind them. George looked at his father. He hated how much he looked like him. He was in his forties, but the man still looked good. He was fit, his clothes well-ironed, and neat. Everything about looked him looked good, he looked exactly just as George could remember him as a boy. He always seemed to have everything in control. However, the eyes. They were different. They were deep, and he looked away, refusing to see anything in them.

"George," Antonio said, taking a step towards his son.

"I don't want you here," George said coldly.

However, he was so stubborn that he placed a hand on George's face. Warning himself, George looked up, and couldn't look away. There was so much sadness in his father's eyes. A tear slid down his father's face, and George could not help the tears that began to drop from him as well.

"I hate you so much," George blurted.

108

"I know. I know son. I hate myself as well," his father said.

"Why? Why did you leave? Why did you hate me so much? Why did you ruin my life? You left me with her! With her!" George yelled.

Luka withdrew from him. He walked over to a chair and dragged it to George. He sat by him, tears in his eyes. "I wish I didn't. I regret everything George. I wish I had fought for you. But I was too stupid. Too young. And when I decided to, it was too late."

George laughed bitterly. Just excuses. "You should have never left. You caused all of it. Broke our family. Drove her crazy!"

"I wish I didn't, but your mother, she... she was driving me over the edge. She was always suspicious about everything I did, everywhere I went. I didn't set out to break our family. But I needed a break from her antics. I never planned to fall in love with another woman, but I did. I admit it, I was selfish. But I wanted to be genuinely happy."

"You were never happy with my mother?" George asked.

Antonio shook his head. "I loved her in a way, but more as a friend. And then she got pregnant, and I felt the right thing to do was to get married, but it was a huge mistake. I kept on holding on for years, hoping that we could save our marriage, but it was doomed from the day we got married. Leaving you was the worst mistake of my life. I tried to fight for you! I tried!"

George looked away.

"Believe me George, but she wasn't willing for me to have custody. I sought for joint custody but it was refused as well. I decided to deal with the few moments I had with you, but every time I came around..."

"She would ruin it for us," George said quietly. He remembered how he often looked forward to having his father around, but his mother would always chase him.

"I took her to court, but she fed the authorities with lies why I shouldn't have custody. I couldn't stand being around her, and all that negativity. I just... gave up. Hoping time would work things out."

"You were wrong, you both messed up my life, destroyed the childhood I never had," George said quietly.

"I have no excuse for leaving George, but I tried to reach out. I sent letters, I sent gifts, but I got no response. I thought you didn't want to have anything to do with it. I felt... I deserved it. For leaving."

George knew his father wasn't lying about the letters, he was pretty sure his mother had gotten rid of them. That was how much she hated his father.

"I'm sorry son, for not being there, for being a deadbeat father. You have no idea how much I hate myself every day. I have never stopped thinking of you. Never!"

George didn't like the feeling that was overwhelming him. He had never known all this while that his father had cared. His father had been horrible for abandoning him, but did he really blame him? With how awful his mother was? No sane person could deal with his mother, he had tried, and he had turned out broken.

There was a knock on the door, and without getting an answer, the person walked in. George's eyes widened in surprise when he saw who it was.

"Anton! What on earth are you doing here?"

TEARS IN THE MIST

He ignored the pain he felt and hugged his friend tightly. He could feel the tears in his eyes but he reined them. There were too many tears already shed for the day. When he pulled apart from his friend, he had so many questions. Anton looked good, he had added some weight and was now burly, and he looked quite mature, but he looked like the Anton who had been his friend.

"It's good to see you, George! We thought you were dead," Anton said.

George' eyes shifted from his father to Anton. There was a familiarity between them, they weren't strangers.

"What are you talking about?" George asked.

For the next hour, both men told him a long tale. When Anton returned home more than a year ago, he was worried about his friend who he had lost touch with. He reached out to the Archbishop in Australia who not only gave him negative reports about George but informed him that he had returned home to Greece. Alessandra had had no idea where he was and had shown Anton out the door, calling him names. No one had seen George or knew where he was. Worried, Anton had stormed into Antonio's office and had demanded to know where George is.

"I had no idea where you were either," Antonio said. "It was a wakeup call for me. We both began to look for you, but no one had seen you. We checked the hospitals, the morgue, even filed a police report, but they weren't willing to help. We figured you didn't want to be found, or worse, you were dead. We haven't stopped looking for you, although I must admit, I began to lose hope. You have no idea how stunned I was to see you yesterday. I thought all this while, that something horrible had happened to you. I'm so sorry George. I know my apologies can never make up for the past…" Antonio's voice broke, sending sadness through George. He patted his father on the shoulder, the closest he could summon himself to do.

"Where on earth have you been George? This… I didn't expect to see you dressed as a homeless man. Didn't know that was your thing," Anton teased, trying to liven the mood.

George sighed. Where on earth was he going to start from? Anton gave him an encouraging smile. "I messed up George, I shouldn't have cut our bond, but I had a lot going. Not an excuse, but we're here. Your dad and I. I know you have gone through a lot, but it's time. It's time for it to end."

"I'm broken," George said. He went on to tell them all that had happened, from the moment his father had left, what had happened in Australia and his return to Greece. There was fury in his father's and friend's faces when he was done. His father got up and hit the wall, making George startle in fear.

"That bastard!" Antonio growled, his eyes red with fury.

"I…"

"Don't blame it on yourself. Don't you dare," Anton snapped. "I should have known he was up to no good when you fell off the grid. I just assumed that your priestly duties demanded you cut ties with me. Don't be an ashamed friend, don't hate yourself. You did nothing wrong. He's the messed up one here."

"He's going to pay," Antonio said with a cold smile which sent a chill through George. The look vanished and he looked at his son with sadness. "There's so much I wish I could take away. There's so much I wish you didn't go through. But now, I am here. We're here. You have a new family, siblings, and I know it's all alien to you, but I want to take that suffering away from you. You have gone through a lot son, no one should go through this.

112

Yesterday... it was a miracle. You saved your brother. This life is twisted, and I have no idea how it freaking works, but we met again. This is not a coincidence, this is you starting afresh, and this is you moving on."

George was in awe of all that had happened since the previous day. With just one encounter, in one day, his life had changed. When he had awakened yester morning, he had had no idea that he would save a life, nevertheless reunite with his father. Life was a freaking mystery. He didn't know if to be happy or sad, that Christ had made his life turn out this way, but for the first time in forever, he was glad to be alive. The words came out of his mouth without restraint. "I forgive you, father," he said.

Warm arms surrounded him. They didn't repulse him or make him want to fight out in rage. They only comforted him, taking him to a time when a hug from his father meant no harm was ever going to happen to him. Although he had demons, he could tell that he was safe.

"Thank you, son," Luka whispered. "Now we rebuild."

RETRIBUTION

The door clicked behind him and he took the elevator to the fifth floor. It had been a long day for George, and he needed to have a warm bath and have some rest. First, he had been at the office till evening, then spent about an hour with his therapist. When his father had suggested a therapist months ago, George had been against it. It was enough he had told him and Anton the truth, but telling a stranger? It had seemed absurd. However, it was of great help. He still had the nightmares but they came once in a while and were not as bad as before. He refused to blame himself anymore for what the bastard had done to him, as well as his mother. He still hadn't forgiven the Archbishop; that past, that bitterness, he still held on to, and he had told the therapist that he doubted he would. It was a hatred he would take to his grave.

The apartment he stayed was a gift from his father, the deed signed in his name. Over the years, Antonio had done a lot for himself and worked as an independent constructor, who dabbled in government deals. At times, George wondered what could have happened if he had just put his pride and anger aside, and sought for his father. But as his therapist had said, there were no "ifs". What had happened was in the past, there was no way he could undo them. He needed to focus on what the future held.

Now, he was in a better place. He worked in a charity organization, and he was at the front of it, making sure that the less privileged were cared for. It was a huge project for him. He had been on the other side and knew how it felt to be homeless and without a penny. He didn't work in his priesthood capacity, although it did come to light whenever he interacted with others. Although he despised that institution and didn't want to be a part of it, it would always reflect in his way of life. He could not recall the last time he had stepped into a church, and he doubted he would for the rest of his life. He had a relationship with Christ, and that was enough, but for the church? He had seen enough to last him a lifetime.

He lay on a couch after an early dinner, the TV on. He was more thoughtful nowadays, and it had to do with his life out there. He had changed a lot in his looks since he had left the hospital. He had trimmed his beard and his hair, and he had added some weight. No one would be able to compare the homeless man to how he looked now. Yet, he was still growing, trying to get a hang of his new life.

His relationship with his family was one he deeply appreciated. He and his dad, Antonio, had established something, they were building a relationship he cherished. Artemis, his stepmom was an amazing woman. He had been quite suspicious of her at the onset, assured that she was just like his mother, but she was a caring woman, who loved his father and cared for him as well. He had three siblings, and while it seemed strange having younger ones, he knew he would go the mile for them.

As for his mother, it had been a long while since he had last seen her. He and Antonio had paid her a visit when he left the hospital. She had been calm at first but had flared up afterward, demanding that the conniving bastards leave her house. He knew she was sick, she had always been, but his father departure only worsened her state. He had employed a help for her, but she had scratched her eyes. She didn't want his help. She didn't want him around, and as much as it hurt him to see her hate him so much, he could deal with it. He had been hurt so much already, one more rejection wouldn't kill him. He just hoped that someday, she would be willing to move on.

His friendship with Anton was at the best level possible. It was as if they had never drifted apart. Anton was done with his education and was now surprisingly working with the state legal department. He never would have figured out his friend for the suit and tie type. But then, Anton had gotten matured, with life teaching him a few lessons.

He still was getting the hang of socializing with others. He had just a few friends, mostly from the charity whom he warmed up to. As for his encounter with the opposite sex, he was still shy, but he had gone through a few sexual encounters without being revolted, although it had taken a while getting used to. He still had a long way to go, but at least, he was headed towards development.

His eyes lifted to the TV screen. It was news hour. He didn't increase the volume, but his eyes were on the headline which caught him by surprise. "Visiting Archbishop James Nikkolopoulos gone missing". The Archbishop had arrived the night before and had gone missing earlier in the afternoon. The cops were looking for him, but so far, there were no leads to who had kidnapped the Archbishop. George rolled his eyes, distaste suddenly filling him up. The bastard had the nerves to come into town and the church would, of course, be throwing some banquet for him. The stupid lot of them. He was sure he was in some brothel with some young man, whose life he was about to ruin. The hatred he felt for him returned in full force.

George's phone rang. It was his father. A short text. His eyes narrowed. What was the man on about? He grabbed his jacket and headed out to a dark taxi which was waiting. The taxi drove to the other side of town, filled with rundown factories, and homes covered with graffiti. He wondered what his father had decided to cook up in the middle of the night, and in such area.

The car finally stopped in front of an abandoned warehouse which was very quiet, with no source of light. The car waited, as George knocked on the door. It was opened by Kasey, his father's second in command, and cousin. He was a thin gaunt man with a smile which was always affectionate. However, tonight, he had on a solemn look.

"Where's Antonio?" George asked.

He followed Kasey who led him deeper into the building which reeked of dust, with roaches and rats crawling about.

George stopped at the scene before him. Seated in front of a chair, his hands tied to the back, and a bag over his head was a man. He would know that man anywhere. He had had nightmares of him over the years. Standing in front of the Archbishop was his father, hatred in his eyes. The Archbishop was bloodied, his shirt covered with blood, as well as his boxers.

"What's happening?" George asked as he slid up to his father.

"I told you I would get even. He can't get away with it. No one can," Antonio said. He pulled the bag from over the Archbishop's face.

"George!" the Archbishop said in surprise at the sight of him. "Help me! Help me! They took me! Get some help!"

George glared at the man he hated with so much passion. His nose was broken and stained with blood and mucus. His eyes were red from crying from the pain and pleading. This was the man who had caused him so much pain. The man who had ruined his life, and was now sulking like a baby.

"I should help you? After all, you did to me?" George yelled in the quiet warehouse.

"I'm sorry! I really am! Please help me! Tell them to release me. I promise not to tell anyone," the Archbishop pleaded.

George shook his head. He was a liar as well. The man was not a bit sorry. All he wanted was to be free. He was sure once he was free, he would not only rat out their names to the cops but would find some poor boy to hurt. People like him never changed, they knew that with their power they could get away with anything.

The Archbishop's eyes narrowed as George approached him. He began to jerk on the chair, against his restrains. George looked down at the man. A man he had once cared for and held in high esteem. A man he had once called father and had considered a role model. A man he now hated.

"Please, Father George, help me. For the sake of the Church, for the love of Christ. You took an oath, you're a priest!" the Archbishop cried.

George laughed. How convenient it was for him. "You tried to ruin my life. You tried to make me think I was a no one, and for a while, I believed you. But not anymore."

"Please!" the Archbishop pleaded.

George slapped him across the face, and he became quiet, whimpering quietly.

"What do you want us to do to him?" Kasey asked, a wicked gleam in his eyes. "We can cut that thing that dangles between his legs off, electrify himself, just tell me, son."

"I don't know," George said. He had never expected to walk into this, or that his father would be responsible for kidnapping the Archbishop.

"Take this."

George looked up and took a step back. His father held out a revolver to him. How he got it, he had no idea. But from what he had seen in the past months, his father would move mountains to make sure he was happy. George stretched his hand and took the gun from him.

"No! Please no! George! I cared for you!" the Archbishop pleaded.

The gunshot roared all over the warehouse. It was followed by another, and then another. The body stiffened on the chair, a hole in the head of the Archbishop.

"He will never be found," Antonio said with assurance, the hatred in his eyes.

All George could do was nod. Did he feel better? A whole lot. The worthless soul was gone, and he felt a vacuum filled. He would still be haunted, but he would always take solace that the monster had died by his hand. Finally, he could put the past to rest, and move on. He turned around, got back into the taxi, and headed back home for the new dawn.

Made in the USA
Lexington, KY
16 November 2018